SCARLET PASSION

"Something is wrong here," Steven said as he stepped before her and looked down into her eyes. "Perhaps this time I should leave and not return. Just say the word, Rochelle."

Knowing this was her last chance to make him stay, Rochelle stepped closer to him and placed her lips over his. Her heart thundered wildly as she felt flames of desire rushing through her.

"You're so beautiful," Steven murmured. As he drew her against his hard frame, his lips lowered to hers in a series of sweet, teasing kisses.

Now his fingers wove through the red silk of her hair, and Rochelle no longer cared what was right or wrong. Anything this delicious had to be right. Her body was coming alive for the first time ever and she wouldn't deny herself this pleasure. She was a woman whose needs had been locked inside her for a long time. Now they were being unleashed by this perfect specimen of a man, though he was still her enemy and always would be. But he was an enchanting enemy. . . .

ENCHANTED ENEMY

Cassie Edwards

ZEBRA BOOKS
Kensington Publishing Corp.
http://www.zebrabooks.com

ZEBRA BOOKS are published by

Kensington Publishing Corp.
850 Third Avenue
New York, NY 10022

All Kensington titles, imprints, and distributed lines are available at special quantity discounts for bulk purchases for sales promotion, premiums, fund-raising, and educational or institutional use.

Special book excerpts or customized printings can also be created to fit specific needs. For details, write or phone the office of the Kensington Special Sales Manager: Kensington Publishing Corp., 850 Third Avenue, New York, NY 10022, Attn: Special Sales Department. Phone: 1-800-221-2647.

First Printing: March 1988
10 9 8 7 6 5 4 3

Printed in the United States of America

You kissed me! My head drooped low on your breast
With a feeling of shelter and infinite rest
While the holy emotions my tongue dared not speak
Flashed up as in flame, from my heart to my cheek;
Your arms held me fast; oh! your arms were so bold—
Heart beat against heart in their passionate fold.
Your glances seemed drawing my soul through mine eyes
As the sun draws the mist from the sea to the skies.
Your lips clung to mine till I prayed in my bliss
They might never unclasp from the rapturous kiss.

—*Hunt*

One

May 24, 1861, Alexandria, Virginia

The city was calm as the morning sun tried to break through the patchy fog drifting in from the port of Alexandria. The windows along the streets seemed to be yawning with their shades only partially raised, and tantalizing kitchen aromas drew sleepy risers to their breakfast tables.

Rochelle Jackson hugged her brother, Richard, as he drifted into the dining room, now slipping his suspenders over his shoulders, his green eyes still droopy with sleep.

"Richard, were you up late again reading?" Rochelle scolded, smoothing a lock of hair back from her brother's freckled brow.

Richard gave his sister a beguiling smile, revealing a bright flash of teeth. "If I'm going to be a man of the world, I've got to read about it first, huh, Sis?" he teased, winking.

A flush suffused her cheeks as she cast him a harried look over her shoulder. He assisted her to a chair at the dining table. "Richard, my word!" she whispered harshly. "Such a thing to say!"

As a twin, she saw something of herself each morning when she saw Richard. They had been gifted with the same flame of red hair, the cool green eyes, the tiny-boned frame, each of them only a few inches over five feet tall, but each with as much muscle as any two men, though they were only sixteen. Their wrestling had only recently become taboo for Rochelle because of her transition into womanhood. Until now she had fought as vigorously and skillfully as any boy because her brother challenged her to do so, and Rochelle had never been one to say no to a challenge . . . any challenge.

Yet perhaps the time had come for her to behave like a lady. But why was it taking so long for her to blossom out fully?

She took a quick glance downward and saw the lack of fullness in her breasts. In her cotton dress, gathered full at the waist, she showed no signs, yet, of becoming as well developed as most girls her age. She was sixteen and still she had such a little girl's figure!

But at least she had the gift of beautiful hair: it hung halfway down her back. Some said it was the color of a brilliant burnished rose, all satiny soft. And some compared it to the Virginia sunset, flaming and almost alive.

Suddenly she felt guilty for having worried about such things as her figure, for there were much more important things at stake here in Virginia than what was right or wrong about one girl of sixteen.

War was imminent in the city of Alexandria. Even now Confederate soldiers were billeted all over the city in their own homes, waiting, watching. . . .

Rochelle watched as her father and his best friend and associate, Anthony Oliver, settled down at the breakfast table. She saw the troubled looks on their faces and knew what was on their minds. Wasn't it the same for anyone who loved their city, their homes, their businesses?

The fate of their own Jackson House Inn lay in the hands of the soldiers and their ability to protect the city from the invasion of Union regiments. Many doubted Alexandria could withstand an attack. . . .

"And just what did I hear you say about reading into the wee hours of the morning?" Daniel Jackson asked, eyeing first his daughter and then his son, seeing their looks of uneasiness. He knew his children well enough to know that any of their conversation this day would be calculated to lighten his mood. Teasings about some questionable book had been made only for his benefit, to distract him.

"I'm sure it wasn't a book of poetry." Rochelle smiled wickedly at Richard as he arranged himself beside her. He scooped a heaping mound of scrambled eggs into his plate, purposely ignoring her.

But then her smile faded; no one commented one way or the other on what she'd just said. She looked mutely from Richard to her father, and then to Anthony. Everyone was intensely solemn; tensions reigned; they all feared the future.

She knew that her father and Anthony had spent more time reminiscing about the past lately than ever before . . . talking over times they had shared when they had lived carefree in Texas, out on the range, mavericking cows. Anthony had been head wrangler for Daniel Jackson. Anthony had even traveled north with Daniel after Daniel's wife had not survived the ordeal of birthing the twins.

Daniel had wanted to see to it that his children were raised on land that was tame and where they would have all opportunities of a proper education. The decision to travel with Daniel hadn't been all that hard for

Anthony, for he had been injured while mavericking. The physical scars had healed, but not those festering inside. He had lost a bit of grit that day on the range, something which only time could replace. . . .

"There's no gettin' around talk of what's happening in the country today," Daniel said, pouring himself a cup of coffee. "No talk of poetry can make us forget what the true topic of conversation is at every breakfast table this mornin'."

"Secession, Father?" Rochelle asked, sipping from a glass of orange juice.

"Yes. Seccession," Daniel grumbled, his faded green eyes full of worry. "Only yesterday Virginia voted in a popular referendum and ratified a previous convention vote in favor of secession from the Union, making our state a member of the Confederacy. You know Lincoln ain't going to stand for it. Rochelle, it'd been best had I stayed in Texas to raise you and your brother."

Richard toyed with his fork, then looked at his father, seeing the pallor of is face and the purple hue of his lips. His father's hair had only recently thinned. And it was all because of Lincoln and his determination to have things his way. The worry was aging Richard's father almost overnight, it seemed.

"I'm glad we're here in Virginia," Richard said smugly. "Just let Lincoln send Bluebellies here to fight. I'll show 'em a thing or two, Father."

"All I've ever wanted was peace," Daniel sighed. "I thought I'd found it here many years ago. I had mavericked myself out. It was nice buyin' this inn and managing it. Now who's to say how long it will be ours?"

Rochelle's eyes widened. "No one can take our inn from us," she said in a rush of words. "Surely you don't think they'd try!"

Anthony reached over and patted Rochelle's tiny hand. "No . . . no one's going to take anything from you if *I* have anything to say about it," he vowed. "Don't fret so, Rochelle—it could make your hair turn gray. Now you don't want that to happen before you even catch yourself a man, do you?"

Laughing softly, Rochelle smiled over at Anthony, glad to have him as a special friend. Though he favored peace as much as his best friend, Daniel, Rochelle truly believed he would fight to the death for her, or any of the rest of the family. His loyalties ran deep. He was a true friend, and not only that—he was handsome.

She had just begun to realize how attractive he was and wondered why he hadn't married. He was the age of her father! Was he the sort who chose bachelorhood over marriage? If so, she couldn't understand why. He surely could have any woman he desired. If she were twenty years older, she would certainly take notice of such fine features on a man.

He was all muscle and sinew, of medium height, and was as gentle as her father. But she knew her love for him would always be that of a daughter for a father. . . .

"What Rochelle needs is one of those Zouave's photographs to dream and swoon over," Richard teased, once more trying to put up a lighthearted front for his father's sake. "From what I hear there's one photograph selling like wildfire. Colonel Ellsworth, I believe is his name. He's supposed to have very black, wavy hair, something the girls are going wild over."

Richard gave Rochelle a look filled with mischief. "Wouldn't you like a photograph of one of those men in funny, baggy red breeches who call themselves soldiers?" he further teased. "They say this Ellsworth's name is synonymous with patriotism to millions of Northerners."

"Richard, please," Rochelle argued. "I know of whom you are speaking, and I care little to hear more. I'm aware of this man's reputation though I am *not* one of the girls who have seen a photograph of him."

"But, Rochelle, Colonel Ellsworth has modeled his unit of Zouave Cadets after the exotic French Zouaves of Crimean War fame," Richard further teased. "From what I've heard, he's developed his own variations of the Zouave drill, featuring hundreds of swift and sometimes acrobatic maneuvers with musket and bayonet."

"There's more to that man than to tease about," Daniel interjected. "He's built himself quite a reputation fast. It's common knowledge that Ellsworth campaigned for Lincoln durin' the presidential election. He even accompanied the President-elect to Washington as his bodyguard and confidant and became Lincoln's close friend."

"Yes, this man is said to be the Union's most promising military talent," Anthony said, giving Daniel a sour look. "Despite the baggy-trousered uniforms, Ellsworth's group of soldiers are not to be taken lightly."

"How could you see him as anything but foolish, knowing how he formed his regiment?" Richard asked scornfully, brushing his half-eaten dish of scrambled eggs away from him. "Why, he was a commander of the United States Zouave Cadets. All he did was transform them from a spiritless group of Chicagoans into a national-champion drill team. Does this warrant all the attention he has somehow managed to get?"

"He proved his worth by touring the cities in the East, challenging all comers to compete against his Zouaves," Anthony shrugged. "He became a celebrity overnight. Editorial writers lionize him, women swoon over him, and politicians seek his friendship. Abraham

Lincoln has been known to have called him the greatest little man that he has ever met."

"Hogwash!" Rochelle chided. "I agree with Richard. The baggy-pants men who call themselves soldiers are surely nothing but a bunch of pansies."

"Just let 'em come to Alexandria," Richard scoffed. "I'll show 'em what good old-fashioned shooting is all about. I need none of that fancy stuff to get my point across where guns are concerned."

A rush of footsteps drew all attention to the door. James, a neighbor boy of fourteen, stood there breathless, his face etched with fear.

Daniel pushed his chair back and quickly rose. He went to James and placed his hands on his shoulders. "Lad, what is it?" he asked, fearful. James's face was flushed and his eyes were wild. In his right hand he clutched an Enfield rifle.

"Through the fog I saw 'em," James said. He looked from Rochelle to Richard, who still sat at the table speechless. He looked up into Anthony's steel-gray eyes as he came to stand beside Daniel.

"You saw what?" Anthony queried, frowning. "Get hold of yourself, James. What did you see? Tell us."

"Four ships, headed for port," James said in a rush of words. "No. I mean to say I saw three river steamers and one sloop-of-war, the *Pawnee*, as the steamers' escort."

Daniel's hands dropped to his side. He paled. "Good Lord," he said shallowly. "It's happening just as I feared. The town and everything in it will soon be under Union command."

Richard knocked his chair over backward in his rush to get to his feet. He went to his father and faced him boldly. "Father, it sounds like you've given up without a fight," he gasped. "We can't give up everything that easily. By damn, I'm going to fight!"

Daniel placed a hand heavily on his son's shoulder. "Son, I've always been a peace-loving man," he said softly. "I didn't ask for war. But yes, we must defend what's ours."

Daniel then turned and looked wearily toward Rochelle. "Come with me, Daughter," he said thickly. "We must get you hidden before the soldiers get here. At least *you* can be spared."

"Father, there won't be any place safe for Rochelle," Richard argued.

Daniel frowned. "Son, we must at least try," he said. "I'll get her upstairs while you keep watch down here."

Anthony nodded toward James. "Go on your way, lad," he encouraged. "Spread the word." He looked at Daniel. "I'll go outside and take a look. Richard, don't do anything in haste. Life is too easily snuffed out with a bullet."

"I can damn well take care of myself," Richard said smugly. "Nothing is going to happen to me or to any of you."

As Daniel ushered Rochelle out into the hallway, he looked at the scene around him. He was glad the inn wasn't inhabited this day. The talk of unrest had at least done him that favor. It had scared people into staying home, instead of gadding about. He didn't have anyone but his family to be concerned about when the need to protect them was greatest.

Anthony hurried on out into the gray day. Though the fog was lifting, the sun was still struggling to break through clouds which lay heavily over the city. He stepped out onto the cobblestones and peered toward the river. It was too hard to tell yet, because of the fog still swirling there, whether or not the ships had docked.

Then something else drew his quick attention. His heart skipped a beat when his gaze moved upward and saw the boldness of the Confederate flag flying from the upper story of his friend's inn. . . .

He started to go to warn them that this could draw undue attention to their establishment, but then a rush of feet caught his attention. His insides froze: Alexandria's own Confederate troops, a sprinkling of Virginia militia, were hurriedly leaving town, heading toward the railroad station. Anthony knew that his friends needed him, but without the militia to fight for the whole town, all would be lost.

He began running toward the soldiers, hoping to be able to talk some sense into the cowardly bastards. Surely they didn't want to forever be branded as cowards. . . .

Standing shoulder-to-shoulder at the *Pawnee*'s leeward rail, Colonel Elmer Ellsworth and Corporal Steven Browning watched as the sloop-of-war edged closer to the wharf. Steven Browning was proud to be a part of Colonel Ellsworth's regiment of Zouaves. Colonel Ellsworth stood for all that was right in the world. And when word had been received of Virginia's secession from the Union, and that Federal troops had been ordered to cross the Potomac River to seize the critical points on the Virginia side, it had been Colonel Ellsworth who had wangled this choice objective for his Zouaves . . . the port city of Alexandria.

Both Colonel Ellsworth and Corporal Browning were dressed in resplendent new uniforms for the planned assault. They wore navy blue coats, red bloomered breeches, tight leggings, and red caps with black bills.

Pinned on their chests were gold medals inscribed in Latin with the words, "Not for ourselves alone but for country."

Steven stiffened at the clanking of chains, proof that the anchor was now being lowered and that soon they would be leaving the ship. He had anxiously awaited the moment he would fight alongside such a well-respected man as Elmer Ellsworth, yet word had been received that a warning had been sent ahead by none other than a naval officer from the *Pawnee*. Now no one knew what to expect in Alexandria; no one knew the strength of the Confederate forces. It wasn't that Steven was afraid; this was his very first introduction into battle . . . battle of any sort. And the word to describe his feelings was that of great excitement.

He had felt the need to fight for what he believed in. Lincoln's beliefs were his beliefs, and he would fight to the death for the preservation of such rights.

Standing handsomely tall, broad-shouldered, and thin-flanked, Steven looked the picture of dignity as he eagerly awaited the orders to leave the ship. Fair-skinned, he was now rugged with freckles on his high cheekbones and proud, straight nose. His blue eyes were piercing; his shoulder-length blond hair had bleached out to a dull yellow. When he spoke it was in a soft, gentle drawl, though his mavericking since the age of twelve had made him a man of brawn and stamina.

"What harm to you think has been done by word of our arrival getting there before us?" he asked, placing a hand on his rifle. Colonel Ellsworth's dark eyes scanned the wharf, sensing it to be too quiet. Then he focused his attention on Steven.

"I still can't understand how any naval officer could go without authorization to the commander of the Alexandria garrison to offer a truce," Colonel Ellsworth said firmly. "The truce offered Colonel George H. Terrett could not be accepted as official, having been offered by just one man. Surely Terrett knows this and can still expect us to come and do our duty."

"Not used to the thought of war yet, the naval officer seemed to be doing what he thought was best," Steven said dryly. "His motive was to spare the women and children of the city any risk of gunfire."

"We all want to spare the women and children," Colonel Ellsworth argued, grasping the saber at his side. "But such negligent warnings can cause more deaths than save lives."

"I'm sure the officer understands now," Steven said. He looked toward shore. Because of the lingering fog, he was unable to make out much in the distance. He leaned against the rail, squinting. "Colonel Willcox's First Michigan Regiment should be marching into town from the north just about now. As soon as our Eleventh New York Regiment goes ashore from the ship, it shouldn't take too long to meet halfway."

"That's what we hope for," Colonel Ellsworth said, moving away from the ship's rail as the gangplank was lowered to the wharf. "It's time, Steven. Let's go and show Alexandria just why our regiment was chosen to seize their fair city."

Colonel Ellsworth dispatched one company of soldiers to take the railroad station, while he and a small detachment set off to capture the telegraph office. Only a few shots were exchanged with the vanishing rear guard of the Confederate regiment. Most had already fled on railway cars and only thirty-five dawdling Rebel horsemen were captured.

A few blocks up King Street, Colonel Ellsworth came to an abrupt halt. Steven's gaze followed Colonel Ellsworth's, now seeing his cause to stop in mid-step.

"A Confederate flag," Steven said beneath his breath. His gaze moved slowly over the three-story brick building, seeing the name engraved in stone over the front door. "Jackson House Inn," he murmured. "Whoever is the proprietor seems not to have heard of our invasion. Who would be so bold as to continue to fly the Confederate flag after being warned?"

"The Confederates are a loyal lot," Colonel Ellsworth said bluntly. "Just as we are loyal, Steven, to the Union cause."

"What are we to do about the flag?" Steven asked, grasping harder onto his rifle, ready for a fight.

"Do you even have to ask?" Colonel Ellsworth said, his face stern. "I want that flag taken down *immediately.*"

"As good as done," Steven said, walking confidently beside the colonel as they hurried toward the inn.

Colonel Ellsworth stationed guards on the first floor of the inn, then dashed upstairs with four comrades, Steven among them.

Richard heard the rustling of feet and the drone of low voices. He was on the second floor of the inn, hiding beneath the stairwell. He grabbed his shotgun and raced to first check that Rochelle was safe before confronting the Union men.

He breathed easier at seeing that Rochelle and his father were safe in the bedroom; he went to Rochelle, placed an arm about her waist, and drew her into his embrace, holding the shotgun away from her.

"Sis, you stay here with Father," he said. "Soldiers

are in the inn. They went on upstairs. I'm going to catch them cold when they come back down."

Daniel reached for his rifle. "I'll go with you, Son," he said. "I can't let you face the danger alone."

Richard looked heavy-lidded toward his father. "No, Father," he pleaded. "You stay here with Rochelle. I can take care of this. I'm sure there are only a few of them."

"It was the flag," Daniel worried. "They saw the flag. I knew we should've taken it down."

"No—we shouldn't have," Richard argued. "That flag stands for what we believe in."

"But, Son, don't you see? For now it's over," Daniel said hoarsely. "You don't hear any gunfire, do you? Seems Colonel Terrett has deserted his command, or you'd hear something. Perhaps it's best if you place your gun aside. The Union officers surely won't take arms against a defenseless innkeeper?"

"I'm no coward," Richard argued. "I will defend our inn, as I will defend you."

Daniel placed a hand on Richard's shoulder. "I'm no coward either, Son," he said. "But there is a time to realize it is best not to show arms."

Daniel looked from his own rifle to Richard's shotgun. "Son, place the gun aside," he further encouraged. "Let's let whoever is here do what they feel they must, which I am sure is only to remove the flag. Then let them go on their way. It's the peaceful way, Son."

Richard jerked away from his father. He gave Rochelle a lingering look, then rushed from the room and out into the hallway, to crouch in a dark corner to wait. . . .

After cutting down the flag, Colonel Ellsworth and the rest of his comrades started back down the stairs, preceded by Steven. At the second floor landing, Richard stood waiting with his double-barreled shotgun leveled at them.

Instinctively Steven batted the shotgun with the barrel of his musket, but Richard proceeded to pull the trigger. Colonel Ellsworth was immediately hit. Steven watched, mortified, as his leader dropped forward with the heavy, horrible weight that always accompanied sudden death.

And then, aware that the shotgun was now pointed in his direction, Steven looked Richard's way just as Richard fired his second barrel, and luckily missed.

Steven then fired simultaneously and hit Richard flush in the chest. And as Richard crumpled to the floor, Steven again acted with instinct and bayoneted Richard's body, sending it crashing down the stairs.

Rochelle had heard the first gunfire and had rushed to the door and opened it just in time to see Richard grab for his chest and crumple to the floor. As though frozen, she watched further as a bayonet penetrated her brother's chest. Screams filled the air and Rochelle was suddenly aware that they were her own. She covered her ears, trying to deaden the terrible, heart-wrenching sound. But nothing could erase the death scene from her eyes, which were still transfixed on her brother's body as it tumbled down the stairs, lifeless.

And then her eyes moved upward. She found herself looking into the eyes of the man who had just taken her brother's life. She wanted to rush to the soldier, pound her fists against his chest, somehow send him also plummeting to his death. But a loud gasp surfacing from behind her made her forget for the moment the thought of revenge, for it was her father who was now in need of her attentions.

Spinning around, she emitted another soft cry at finding her father slumping to the floor, clutching his chest, the gray ashen color of death already beginning to mask his face, his heart the cause.

"No!" Rochelle cried, dropping to her knees beside her father. "Please, no, Father! Not you too!"

She cradled his head in her lap as he labored over his last breaths. "Anthony. Let . . . Anthony . . . look after you, Rochelle," her father whispered. "He looks to you . . . as a father does. He will see to . . . your welfare. . . ."

Tears streamed down her face. She placed her cheek low against her father's. When his last breath was taken, she whispered a silent vow to him. "Father, I will somehow make the man who is responsible for this pay," she sobbed. "Somehow, he will pay."

She felt empty . . . utterly empty. In only a matter of moments, her world had been torn apart, and she was now alone, except for the beloved Anthony. But that wasn't enough. Losing her father was hard to bear. But without her twin brother, she feared that she would never feel more than half-alive. . . .

Two

Rochelle arranged a double funeral for her father and brother and was glad when the sorrowful day finally passed. The Confederate coroner had ruled that Richard had been killed in defense of his home and private rights; only the Northerners condemned him. He had killed the famous Colonel Elmer Ellsworth . . . the man who meant so much not only to the North, but also personally to Abraham Lincoln.

Rochelle slipped the black veil from her head and the black velvet cape from her shoulders, revealing her stark, black, full-gathered dress. She felt her mourning would never end, for she wasn't sure if she could go on without her brother and father.

Setting her lips in a stubborn straight line and flinging her hair back from her shoulders, she strode to a table in the parlor and picked up a photograph, staring angrily down at it. "I *must* go on," she whispered. "I *must* be strong. For I have something that needs to be done, and only *I* can do it. I promised Father that the man wouldn't get away with it. Hero? As I see Corporal Steven Browning, he is already dead."

Steven Browning, the soldier who killed Richard, had been promoted to second lieutenant in the Regular

Army, and many photographs of him were being sold as *cartes postal,* treating him as a hero.

Hate swelled within Rochelle as she studied the photograph. Oh, how smug he looked posed on the Confederate flag that had been captured from her father's inn.

Yet, the blood that had stained the flag made her smile, for she knew that that had been Colonel Ellsworth's blood.

But when she looked at the bayonet on Browning's gun, a part of her heart seemed to be tearing away, knowing just whom the bayonet had been used on.

She held the photograph closer, studying every feature of the man she had decided to kill. Though she couldn't tell the color of his eyes from the sepia print, she remembered their piercing blue and the shock that had been registered in them after his commander had been killed.

"When he sees me, surely he won't remember me," she mused. His eyes had met hers for only a brief instant, and even then he hadn't truly seen her. He had obviously been in a state of shock over the death of his fallen hero.

Again Rochelle silently gazed down at the photograph. The more she studied it, the less smugness she saw in his expression. Wasn't there almost a softness about his eyes? The slope of his jaw seemed gentle.

Something mellowed inside her, now seeing how handsome he was. . . .

Suddenly throwing the photograph across the floor, she slumped into a chair and buried her face in her hands. "What am I thinking?" she sobbed. "How can I let myself feel anything but hatred for the man who shot my brother and caused my father to have a heart attack? I must be . . . losing my mind . . ."

"No. You are only behaving as one does who is torn with emotion," Anthony said suddenly as he stepped into the parlor.

Rochelle looked up, seeing him through a blur of tears. "Anthony!" she gasped, feeling herself paling. "How long have you been standing in the doorway? How much did you see . . . and hear?"

Anthony went to the liquor cabinet to pour two glasses of port. He knew that although Rochelle was too young to drink, she needed something now to calm her nerves.

Glancing sideways, he saw the photograph of Steven on the floor. He had earlier wondered why she had wasted money on it. Now he knew: when she'd discovered whom Richard had killed and realized that even the President openly mourned for the man, that was the last straw. He understood how she could wonder about a country that would openly mourn the loss of one man, and not another who was just as fine.

Anthony, dressed neatly in a black wool frock coat and breeches, turned to Rochelle and handed her a glass of port.

"Anthony, Father always said. . . ."

"These aren't ordinary circumstances. Drink it, Rochelle. You need something to calm your nerves. You need something to help clear your head."

"And wine will do both at once?" she softly laughed, accepting the tall-stemmed glass.

"Ah, it has already worked without you having taken even a sip," Anthony said, smiling warmly at her. "Now wasn't that a laugh I just heard?"

Rochelle lowered her eyes, feeling guilty for having laughed. How could she, when the graves were still fresh in the cemetery?

Then she looked up again At Anthony, who was now

her lifeline, it seemed. She could feel the special bond being formed between them and hoped that he would understand her need to avenge her brother's and father's deaths. She knew that Anthony was a peace-loving man, just as her father had been, yet surely he would understand the sore festering inside her, waiting to be healed by action . . . action that would snuff out the life of the man who had so unmercifully shot and then bayoneted her brother to death!

"I must go to Colonel Ellsworth's funeral," she blurted, without any further thought as to what Anthony would say to such a declaration. She had made up her mind. She had her plans and she would carry them out, with or without Anthony.

Anthony jumped, startled, splashing wine over the rim of his glass. He hurriedly sat down in a chair opposite Rochelle, his face shadowed with worry.

"What did you say?" he asked. "Surely I heard wrong. You didn't say that you wanted to attend Colonel Ellsworth's funeral, did you?"

"That's exactly what I said," Rochelle replied, looking down at the wine, deciding not to drink it after all. She placed the glass on the table beside her chair, then rose to her feet and walked to the window. It was another gray day in May.

Anthony placed his wineglass beside hers, then went to Rochelle. He took her tiny hand gently and turned her to face him. "It doesn't make sense, Rochelle," he murmured. "Why on earth would you want to go to that man's funeral? If not for him . . ."

Rochelle lowered her eyes and shook her head. "I know," she said softly. Then her eyes shot up and she looked determinedly at him. "Don't you see, Anthony? Only by going to the funeral will I be able to . . . to avenge the useless deaths of my father and brother."

"I now know what has been on your mind," Anthony said. "But you must forget such foolishness. You can't make others pay for the deaths in your family. All this hate building inside you can only harm you, child. Place it behind you. No good ever comes from hate."

Swinging away from him, Rochelle went and retrieved the photograph from the floor. Again she looked at it, knowing what had to be done. "No matter what you say, I must go to that funeral," she insisted.

Anthony refilled his wineglass and swallowed two fast gulps. He then again went to Rochelle, frowning. "You haven't said what it is you plan to do once you get to the funeral," he said. "You know that even to enter the White House for the funeral could be next to impossible."

Rochelle smiled coyly up at him. "Even for a distant cousin of Colonel Ellsworth?" she said, clasping harder onto the photograph, almost already feeling victorious. She had planned this well. Nothing could go awry. Nothing! Only by getting her revenge could she truly go forward in her life, to begin planning a future for herself without her brother and father. Anthony was a dear, dear man, but never a substitute for the loved ones she had lost. She had only to think of Corporal Browning to remember that he had been the one to alter her future, and now it would be she who would alter his. . . .

"You are aware that the death of Colonel Ellsworth has now a part in all the northern sermons, editorials, songs, and poems, lamenting his loss and proclaiming his heroism, aren't you, Rochelle?" Anthony tested, putting the glass down inside the liquor cabinet.

"Yes, I know these things," Rochelle said lightly, arching an eyebrow. "Why do you ask? What does any of that have to do with what I plan to do?"

"No one who is a threat even to his *body* will be allowed to get near him," Anthony continued. "On President Lincoln's orders, an honor guard took Ellsworth's body to the White House, where it now lies in state, still guarded. What on earth makes you think that going in the guise of a cousin will get you anywhere close to the casket?"

"I will manage," Rochelle said.

"Then I must ask you something," Anthony retorted, having saved the worst question to last. "What are your plans once you get to the funeral? Just what is it that you have on your mind to do, to get your vengeance? You know that I cannot approve of anything that could be dangerous to you in any way, Rochelle."

"There is only one way to rid the earth of such vermin as Corporal Steven Browning," Rochelle said, shrugging.

A dark frown clouded Anthony's face. "And that is . . . ?"

"I plan to take Richard's revolver and use it on Corporal Browning," she said nonchalantly, as though this were a deed she practiced every day.

Anthony grew ashen. He went to Rochelle and clasped her shoulders. "Rochelle, you must be jesting," he said, though he saw a strange determination in the depths of her eyes. "You can't shoot a man. I won't let you. This is no way to solve anything. You can't!"

Rochelle jerked away from him. Her lips were trembling from pent-up emotion. She raked her tiny fingers through the hair at her temples, throwing her head back into a soft cry.

"I can't just do *nothing,*" she cried. "What that man did here . . . here in our inn . . ."

"And the same is being done all over the country in the name of war," Anthony growled. "But lovely young girls like yourself are not taking arms and going after the men who have shot their loved ones. It is not the Christian way, Rochelle. Nor is it the way of a lady. Your father would be ashamed to know you were even thinking of doing such a hideous thing."

Rochelle went to Anthony and placed her face up into his. "And when I spoke of vengeance, just what did you think I had in mind?" she argued.

"What can I say to make you forget such a plan?" Anthony asked, walking away from her, his shoulders slumped in defeat as he settled down into a chair.

"Nothing," she stubbornly stated.

"I can never approve."

"I never asked for your approval."

"You cannot go to the White House alone."

"I can, and I must."

"Then I must be the one to take you there?"

"If not you, I shall go alone."

Anthony hung his head in his hands. "And once there?"

"I will find Corporal Browning."

"And . . . ?"

"I will manage, somehow, to use the gun, Anthony."

He groaned. "You do know that is insane, Rochelle," he sighed.

"War is insane, Anthony. I will only be doing my duty for the Confederacy."

"You are only a young girl of sixteen, Rochelle."

"I feel as though a hundred, Anthony."

"I'm supposed to take care of you. I will be negligent if I let you follow through with this absurd plan of yours."

"Had you rather I sneaked out to do it?"

"You have never been the sort to sneak. . . ."

"As I am not even now, Anthony," she replied, going

to fall to her knees before him where he still sat in his chair. She grabbed his hands and pleaded with her eyes. "Please try to understand, Anthony. Please look to this as something I am doing for the Confederacy if you can't accept the fact that I do it for vengeance."

Anthony shook his head. He lifted a hand to her brow and smoothed her hair back. "If I do approve, it will be for only one reason, Rochelle," he said hoarsely.

"And that reason would be?" she murmured.

"Because I know you better than you know yourself," he said, smiling warmly down at her.

"And how is that?" she asked, leaning her cheek into the palm of his hand as he lowered it to run a thumb down and below the slender curve of her chin. "How can you know me better than I know myself?"

"I know that you could never shoot a man," Anthony said matter-of-factly. "Knowing this is the only way I could approve of you going to the White House to confront this Corporal Browning. Once there, you will see how impossible it is to shoot another human being. Then you will return home, I hope free of this compulsion of yours."

"But what if you are wrong, Anthony?" Rochelle asked. "What if you do agree to take me there and I do pull the trigger? How will you feel about your decision *then* to have aided me in my plan?"

"I have no doubt of the outcome of your visit to the White House," he said smoothly. "I should have thought of it sooner, the fact that you could never do what you plan to do."

Feeling triumphant, if only partially, Rochelle rose to her feet, eager to act. She knew that time was wasting. The funeral for the colonel was to be held this very afternoon. That was why she had seen to her brother's and father's funeral so early in the day. Now the rest of the day was hers, to do what she must.

"Rochelle, the time spent going to the White House could be time spent making true plans for your future," Anthony said, rising, straightening the tail of his coat. "We must talk of what is to be done with this inn. Do you want to sell it . . . perhaps move out of town? We could travel west to Montana. We could leave this damnable war behind us."

With her thoughts swirling as to just what she would say when she found Corporal Browning among the dignitaries at the funeral, Rochelle couldn't be bothered with what was to happen in her life, except for the next few hours.

"Tomorrow," she murmured. "Let's discuss it tomorrow, Anthony. Right now I must ready myself to leave for the White House."

"Anthony shrugged. "Yes, maybe tomorrow would be best," he said. "And I don't know what I was thinking about by mentioning Montana. I only recently heard of the promise of land there. And your father wouldn't want me to take you to such untamed territory. We'll make do here in Alexandria . . . somehow."

Rochelle hugged Anthony tightly to her. "You seem weighted down with the worry of the world just because of me," she whispered. "Anthony, am I going to be such a bother for you?"

"Rochelle, from this day forth, I look to you as my daughter, just as Daniel would want me to," he said hoarsely. He held her back and looked heavy-lidded down at her. "So no more talk of you being a bother, do you hear?"

"If you say so," she sighed.

Anthony chuckled as he stepped back away from her. "If I say?" he said, lifting her chin with a forefinger.

"Have you ever truly listened to anybody? Stubborn as you are, I believe you have pretty much had your say in life. Even your father couldn't tell you much that you didn't already know. And you're only sixteen! What am I to expect in the future?"

Rochelle giggled. "Most of what was done in the past was egged on by Richard," she confessed. "He loved to see me get into all sorts of trouble, teasing and challenging me to do things that made Father's eyebrows raise."

Tears sparkled in the corners of her eyes. "Oh, how I'm going to miss Richard," she whispered, placing a fist to her lips. "The emptiness I already feel is almost unbearable."

Anthony drew her back into his arms and hugged her tenderly to him. "Time heals all wounds," he soothed. "Give it time, Rochelle. You'll see . . . someone will take Richard's place . . . somehow."

"How can anyone replace a brother?" she sobbed. She looked sorrowfully up at him. "He was more than that. He was my *twin.* That makes the loss *double."*

In her heart she was again thinking "revenge," for the loss of a twin made her need to avenge his death even more compelling. In her mind's eye she saw the piercing blue eyes of Corporal Browning. Though she had only a photograph of the man and her vague memory of his features, she knew that she would never forget his eyes; they alone would guide her to him. She had never before seen such blue eyes.

She swung away from Anthony's arms. "I must go," she said. "Time is wasting. . . ."

Rochelle lifted the skirt of her dress and the tail of her cape up into her arms as she ran away from the carriage Anthony sat glowering at her. He still didn't approve, even though he was convinced that she could never harm even a fly. But he had agreed at least to bring her this far, to pacify her sense of what he had decided to call "adventure" for lack of being able to find another word to describe it.

Anthony had decided to wait at the carriage, hoping that Rochelle wouldn't get herself into too much trouble in his absence. Her made-up tale that she was Colonel Elmer Ellsworth's distant cousin might not even get her entrance into the White House. Perhaps the mourners were admitted by invitation only. Then what would she do? Would it be so easy for her to forget her plans and let it all go by the wayside?

Almost gliding up the steep stairs of the White House, Rochelle quickly reached the landing. Seeing uniformed men standing at the wide doorway, she tensed, then moved confidently on, peering through the thin black veil she had chosen to wear, though the hood of her cape completely covered the red flame of her hair.

With her chin lifted confidently, she stepped on past the first uniformed man, but her heart almost stopped when she felt the tight grip of a hand suddenly on her elbow.

"Miss, just where do you think you're going?" a booming voice spoke out from behind her.

Swallowing hard, Rochelle turned slowly around and found herself looking up at a thin man, the blue of his uniform causing hatred to rise inside her. But his gray eyes were kind.

"I've come to attend Colonel Ellsworth's funeral," she said softly, feeling dwarfed by the towering young man.

"Then surely you haven't heard that Colonel Ellsworth's funeral is to be attended only by cabinet members and high military officers, along with the President and his wife, and just a few other personages," the soldier tried to explain.

Rochelle straightened her back. "But, sir, I am a member of the family," she gasped. "Surely the family is admitted."

"Then you should know that the actual burial isn't to be held in Washington today," the man said, bending down closer to her, talking more softly when he saw her reach a handkerchief beneath her veil. He tensed when he heard a soft sniffle.

"Colonel Ellsworth's family waits for his body in New York," he added softly.

"I'm a distant cousin, and I cannot . . . cannot afford . . . the train fare to New York, sir," Rochelle said, again sniffling. "Surely you won't deny me one last look at my cousin."

She tilted her head and looked up at him, lifting her veil so that he could see all of her face. She forced as sincere and sad a look to her face as possible.

The soldier shifted his feet nervously. He looked from side to side. Then he bent low and took her by the elbow, guiding her into the White House. "I see no harm in letting you go inside," he said. "The family should get to pay their last respects. If anyone says anything, just say that Frank gave you permission."

Smiling almost awkwardly down at her, he added, "And what did you say your name was, ma'am?"

Rochelle smiled smugly to herself. "Sir, I didn't," she said, now absorbed in the activity around her. She had been directed into the East Room of the White House. Everyone stood mute, their eyes directed straight ahead, where a casket rested on a carved oaken bier.

The soldier leaned down to whisper into Rochelle's

ear. "Perhaps later you can tell me your name?" he said. "I'd like to see you . . . under more pleasant circumstances."

Rochelle again lifted her veil. She looked directly into the soldier's eyes. "Sir, I am only fourteen," she lied. "And you?"

She sighed to herself as the soldier backed away from her without another word, yet feeling at least good about one thing. This young man had treated her like a woman . . . instead of a flat-chested teenager. Maybe she did have hope for her future after all. Perhaps a man *did* play a part in that future. She had just become too impatient to look older than her years. For a while she had thought that her need to look like a woman was only to please her brother. But now she would have to find out the answer to that question all by herself.

Letting her mind drift back to Richard again made the same old determination swell inside her. She had come here to do what her brother had failed to do. She had come to shoot this Yankee. No matter what Anthony thought, she knew that she could very easily pull the trigger to kill the man who had shot her brother. Just given the chance, yes. And she had even planned it so that she would manage to be alone with Corporal Steven Browning when she shot him. The weight of the pistol tied to her thigh with ribbons was a constant reminder of what must be done. . . .

Rochelle stepped farther into the room of mourners, not yet able to make out any among them except Abraham Lincoln. She had seen several likenesses of him in the newspapers and he was not one to be mistaken for another. He was a man whose features drew attention . . . the magnificence of his eyes, the bold firmness of his nose, the granite chin. He wore a black broadcloth suit and white shirt collar too large for his thin neck; his lips were grim, his hands clasped tightly behind him.

There was a striking beauty to his gray eyes, full, deep, and ineffably tender. It was obvious how grief-stricken he was, reminding Rochelle that Colonel Ellsworth had been his close friend and onetime bodyguard, and the Union's most promising military man.

Feeling a knot forming in her throat, remembering her own grief, Rochelle had to focus her mind elsewhere before going ahead with her plan, not having even yet found Corporal Browning among the crowd of mourners.

She made herself observe the room and how it was furnished. The furniture was gilt and satin in soft pastel colors. Chippendale tables and a gray-and-green Brussels carpet with its design of morning glories showed reflections from the immense crystal chandelier that hung above the casket. Green velvet draperies hung from the ceiling to the floor at the windows.

From somewhere in the distance bells tolled, and from her vantage point Rochelle could see the huge flag of the Union hanging at half-mast just outside the window.

The sight of the flag and the sounds of bells tolling for Colonel Ellsworth made Rochelle decide that too much time had been wasted. She must find Corporal Browning now! She didn't want to stay for the entire funeral. She couldn't bear being forced to show feelings for a man that she hated, even though he lay dead in a casket. . . .

Edging her way through the throng of onlookers, Rochelle began studying faces . . . hair . . . eyes. And then she finally found him. Her heart lurched when she saw Corporal Steven Browning so close she could have reached out and touched him.

She took a quick second glance at him. He looked somewhat different than his photograph, or than how she remembered him from the previous day. This day he wore a full suit of navy blue. He was hatless, displaying hair neatly coiffed to his collar. His finely chiseled features were calm, handsome. His long straight nose and his perfect lips made Rochelle feel a strange swimming sensation in her heart.

And when he turned his eyes in her direction, she didn't see the eyes of horror in penetrating blue that she'd seen last time. She saw now a man whose eyes reached clean into her soul, touching her as no one had before.

She took a clumsy step backward, not understanding this strange phenomenon. She had come here with the intention of remembering the moment he had killed her brother. But somehow this remembrance wouldn't fully materialize. It was as though something was being placed between her and the Corporal. Perhaps it was the voice of her father, telling her not to do anything in haste . . . that this young man had only been doing what was required of him, as Richard had . . . all in the name of the dreaded war.

Rochelle looked away from him, forcing herself to acknowledge that Colonel Ellsworth's heroism would be remembered possibly for centuries to come. Streets, babies, and even towns were being named in his honor. From the Union's grief had sprung a renewed determination against the Confederacy. "Remember Ellsworth" had already become a patriotic slogan.

Bitterness flowed through Rochelle's veins. Her brother, Richard, deserved something of this sort of notice. Hadn't he acted in the name of patriotism, the same as Ellsworth? Those in the South who would consider Richard a hero in his own right were being hushed by the rush of Union troops to the Southern cities, in an effort to stifle more than voices. . . .

Forgetting her moment of weakness when the face of a man had held her awestruck, Rochelle forced herself to begin her planned play-acting. She had come to shoot Corporal Steven Browning, and shoot him she would!

She stepped closer to the casket and looked down onto the waxen face of the dead man. Something grabbed at her insides; suddenly she felt as though she were alone with the deceased in this monstrous room. She couldn't take her eyes from the slight curve of his mouth, nor the wavy gloss of his shoulder-length black hair. It was as though he were only asleep and would suddenly awaken and look accusingly up at her, to tell her that she was not welcome, that it was her brother who had shot him.

She had planned to force a lightheadedness, to feign a fainting spell. But she didn't have to pretend. She was beginning to feel pinpricks of sweat popping out along her brow and above her lip. Her heart was beginning to pound against her ribs. And there seemed to be a haziness drifting across her eyes.

Feeling everything spinning, and suddenly very, very hot, she grabbed at thin air, then sighed with relief when a strong arm was suddenly there, catching her.

Batting her eyes nervously, Rochelle looked up at the one who had rescued her. Her pulse raced and her heart skipped a beat. Corporal Browning was very politely escorting her from the room. His arm slipped about her waist, his voice a soothing, soft drawl as he began speaking gently to her.

"Things will be all right as soon as we get you out of the crowd," he said, walking her down a long corridor, and then toward an empty room. "It was probably the heat. This time of year, it has a way of getting very close indoors, especially when many are gathered in one place."

"Yes, I'm sure that's all it was," Rochelle agreed, wondering, though, how she had let herself get caught up in the viewing of Colonel Ellsworth, letting him affect her in such a way. But his hadn't been the only body she'd viewed this day. There had been her father's and brother's so recently past. That was too much for her to bear in one day, for she'd never ever seen anyone dead before.

Looking about her at the velvet, high-backed chairs, the tapestried windows, and the large oak desk at the far end of the room, she thought she was possibly in President Lincoln's study, or perhaps one of many, the place was so elaborately huge.

But no matter where she was, she was with Corporal Steven Browning, and the opportunity to do as she wished had just been presented to her.

Steven led Rochelle to a chair. He stooped down on one knee before her and tried to see through her veil, wondering why she hadn't dropped the cape back from her hair. No wonder the young girl had become so hot. She was dressed for winter, not for a spring day.

Yet it was obvious that she was in mourning. Perhaps she didn't want anyone to see her tear-streaked face or swollen eyes.

"Now that you are away from the crowd, wouldn't you feel better if you removed the cape and veil?" he asked anyway, wanting to do anything to make her more comfortable. She was so tiny; she couldn't be more than an adolescent.

Panic seized Rochelle. She couldn't let Corporal Browning see her face. What if he remembered her?

They had met eye to eye right after Corporal Browning had shot Richard.

Yet Rochelle remembered that it had all happened very quickly, and Corporal Browning had been in a state of shock. No, surely he wouldn't remember. And wouldn't it be a good test? Maybe it would even be best that he knew who she was just prior to her shooting him!

"Yes, I'm sure you're right," she murmured. She let a hand brush against the skirt of her dress, where beneath it she could feel the hardness of the pistol. Soon . . . she would use it soon.

But first she would take her time. She would savor these moments before her victory!

Very slowly she lifted the veil and deliberately looked directly into his eyes. She saw his face shadow with wonder and his hand lift to touch his chin.

"Have we met before?" he asked, finding his memory clouded by all that had happened these past two days.

"I don't believe so," she said, now slowly letting the hood drop from her hair. She straightened her shoulders and shook her hair to hang loosely down her back.

Steven shook his head, studying her intensely. "I'd swear that we've met somewhere," he said thickly. "Have you attended many functions here at the White House? With whom did you come today?"

"I came on my own," she said, smiling softly, enjoying confusing him. "And, no. I've never been here before. I am only a distant cousin to Colonel Ellsworth. I came to pay my respects . . . that's all."

Steven shrugged. "Oh, well. Perhaps I have confused you with somebody else," he sighed. He took her hand in his and patted it, as one does a child. "Are you better? The ceremony should begin soon."

Rochelle's eyes widened nervously. "No. Not quite yet," she said, again feeling the weight of the pistol against her leg.

Steven settled down on the floor at her feet. "All right, then," he said. "Let's talk awhile. Maybe that will ready you for the rest of the ceremony."

"Yes. That sounds nice," Rochelle murmured, now somehow wanting this; yet his nearness did have an unsettling effect on her. A dull ache knotted within her chest at the thought of actually pulling the trigger on the pistol that would kill this man. Could she do it? If she was going to, why hadn't she already? The longer she waited, the bigger the risk of getting caught. . . .

"Though it may sound like blasphemy to one who is related to such a fine man as Colonel Ellsworth, I can't help but dream of the day the war will be over," Steven said, locking his arms about his knees as he pulled them to his chest.

"Oh?" Rochelle said, sitting more alert, surprised at this confession from such a man at such a time. "And what will you do . . . when the war comes to an end?"

Steven got a faraway look in his heavenly blue eyes. It was as though he was already envisioning exactly where he would like to be at this moment, and that was anywhere but Washington. With Colonel Ellsworth's death had come utter disappointment in what the war represented. But he had made a commitment, and he never backed down on commitments.

"I dream of settling out west—perhaps in Montana," he said thickly. "I would like to have a ranch, with cattle."

Rochelle's heart skipped a beat. She recalled Anthony's desire to go to Montana, to be able to work with cattle again. What a strange coincidence . . . was it perhaps one that could work in her favor? Surely there were other ways to get vengeance than to shoot this man. If she could somehow find out where he would settle after the war, she could follow him there and make life absolutely miserable for him.

"Why Montana?" she dared to ask.

"I've mavericked in Texas. I'd like to try new territory. The land in Montana is opening up. I'd like to try my hand at it."

Then he laughed low and soft. He cast her a half-glance. "But what am I doing?" he said. "This is not the time to talk of such things. Surely you think I'm talking out of my head."

"Not at all," Rochelle said, finding it hard not to reach out to touch him. He seemed so much the touching kind. Almost the same as Richard had been. . . .

Steven rose to his feet and smoothed the tails of his jacket. "I must return to the East Room," he said, reaching for one of Rochelle's hands. He politely kissed it, eyeing her again in a long pause, still wondering where he had seen her. She was one who would not be forgotten easily. Though she was young, her loveliness was radiant; her face blossomed with petal softness; and her soft green eyes were the type that made a heart soar with remembrance.

Yet this was not the time to wonder any longer about it. She was too young for him even to wonder about, much less ask her name. They would never meet again. If they did, it would be years in the future, for he had many battles to fight, and who was to say if he would come through them alive?

Rochelle rose quickly to her feet and half-curtsied toward him. "Thank you for your kindness," she murmured, feeling a blush rise to her cheeks as he continued to look at her studiously. Did he recognize her? If he did, it would be very hard to explain what she was doing here. . . .

"It was my pleasure," Steven said, half-bowing to her, then hurrying on away, leaving Rochelle numb and full of wonder. Nothing had turned out as she had expected except that she *had* met Steven Browning. Now the waiting began; she would make plans to follow his every movement, possibly by means of the newspaper. And if not, she would find out after the war just where he had managed to go. As strongly as he felt about Montana, surely that's what his destination would be.

She must ready herself for the same move. But never could she let Anthony know why. It must appear innocent. Anthony must be led to believe that she had dropped all plans of revenge. Only then could her plan be successful. . . .

Three

The carriage moved down King Street, having left the ferry on the Potomac River behind. Though the city of Alexandria was now occupied by Union soldiers, the freedom to come and go as one pleased hadn't yet been stifled, just as long as one could show that it was for peaceful purposes.

Rochelle slipped the black velvet cape from around her shoulders and then the veil from her face, torn between feeling exhilarated one minute and saddened the next. She hadn't accomplished anything as she had planned, yet she had made contact with Corporal Browning and she knew that had to be enough . . . for now. The war was going to change plans for many, and she was among the selected!

"I didn't hear any gunfire while you were in the White House," Anthony teased as he flicked the reins, sending the gelding on down the street.

Rochelle combed her fingers through her hair, then tossed it back from her shoulders. She cast Anthony a half-glance, seeing his smugness over having known that she could never shoot Corporal Browning. Under different circumstances, in a different, more private setting, she would have!

She sighed disconsolately. "No. I was not afforded the opportunity to do as planned," she said. "I'm sure that makes you happy," she added snippishly.

Anthony's jaw tightened. "Young lady, remember who you are with," he growled. "It is I to whom you will answer until you come of age. Now tell me what happened—all of it."

Rochelle crossed her arms in defiance, frowning, and told him what had happened every inch of the way . . . except for the mention of Montana. That would be her secret for now. Later, much later, Anthony would have a role in her plan . . . *if* she were able to somehow follow Corporal Browning's career.

But she knew that this opportunity would surely be there for her, one way or the other. That was why she had to insist that she continue to live in Alexandria, close to Washington. A man as popular and as important to the militia as Corporal Browning would surely be written and talked about throughout the duration of the war.

"Then you've forgotten this foolishness of getting vengeance?" Anthony said, drawing Rochelle from her moment of thought. "We can now talk of what we're to do with you? Where you're to stay?"

Anthony's last words caused Rochelle to sit upright and her eyes to widen. "What do you mean . . . where I'm going to stay?" she blurted. "I will stay at the inn. Where else?"

"You know that you can't run the inn by yourself," Anthony pointed out. "And I have my own ranch on the edge of town to see to."

"I can hire someone to run the inn," Rochelle said, now stubborn. "Anthony, I must stay there, at least for now. Please understand; I've never lived anywhere else."

He cast her a rueful glance. "Even after what has happened there, you insist on staying?" he asked, then again looked straight ahead, already understanding the difficulty of being a substitute father . . . especially to such a strong-willed young woman as Rochelle!

Her eyes wavered as she remembered the gunfire and the sight of Richard tumbling down the staircase. But that was even more reason not to give up the inn. She had to be forced to remember that fateful day, to keep her mind alert as to what the future held for her. Corporal Browning: she could never forget what she must do to get even. . . .

"I will manage," she muttered, "Anthony, somehow I will manage."

Anthony shook his head, slumped his shoulders and again flicked the horse's reins. When the inn came into view, his insides did a quick flip-flop. His back straightened, his neck thrust out.

"What the . . . ?" he gasped.

Rochelle followed his gaze. All about her heart she felt a strange coldness: a crowd of people stood around the entrance to the inn.

"What are they doing?" she said in a shallow whisper. "Who are they?"

Anthony shouted at the horse and snapped the reins, and soon the carriage pulled to a jerky halt at the curb, as close to the inn as he could get it, the crowd having already taken most of the space in the road with their many horses and buggies.

In a flurry of skirts and petticoats, Rochelle jumped from the carriage and began pushing her way through the throng. She became angry at those who tried to stop her by shoving her sideways. She pushed. She shoved. She used her elbows to get to the door of the inn. And when she rushed on inside, she stopped dead in her footsteps when she realized what was happening.

Placing her hands to her cheeks, she found herself unable to speak from the shock. She watched in utter horror as men and boys were frantically cutting away at her staircase and grabbing pictures from the walls and rugs from the floors.

Finally she found her voice. "What are you doing?" she screamed. "Why are you taking these things? Why are you cutting the staircase away? Get out! Get out! This is *my* inn! You . . . have . . . no right . . . !"

"Lady, I don't care who you are," one man shouted. "We're here to get souvenirs, and by damn, I for one plan to carry some away!"

Rochelle's stomach turned. "Souvenirs . . . ?" she said in a shocked whisper.

Then she began to inch her way through the throng of people, still in a state of shock. She watched in silence as more of her staircase disappeared. A sob caught in her throat when she watched some of her brother's clothes being carried from the inn.

Again she began screaming at them. "*Why* are you doing this? What are your reasons . . . for wanting souvenirs here?"

She grabbed a man by the sleeve. "Sir, listen to me," she cried. "Please stop. Please leave. What you are doing is wrong. Surely you know that!"

The man jerked away from her and gave her a look of utter disgust. "It was your brother who done it, wasn't it?" he said vehemently. "Your brother was the one who shot Colonel Ellsworth?"

Rochelle recoiled in fright. She edged back away from everyone, again wordless.

"I've got a piece of the staircase that has blood on it!" one man said, rushing down the stairs. "Damn if it ain't Colonel Ellsworth's blood. I've surely got the best souvenir of all!"

Now Rochelle understood. Colonel Ellsworth was a fallen hero. Everyone seemed now to regard him as a martyr. They wanted souvenirs because of him. Everyone wanted a memento, not caring that they were defacing property that didn't belong to them.

Anthony rushed into the inn. He began grabbing men by the shirt collar, ushering them back outside, one by one. But his efforts were futile. The more he threw out, the more seemed to come back in.

He went to Rochelle and placed his arm about her waist and guided her to the back of the inn, to a room that was not yet disturbed by anyone.

Rochelle began sobbing. She clung to Anthony, placing her wet cheek against the solid bulk of his chest. "The world has gone crazy," she cried. "I can't believe any of this nightmare, Anthony. What am I to do?"

"As soon as the crowd disperses, you are to go through the inn. Take what is left of importance to you. Then I am going to take you to your Aunt Sara's house."

Rochelle drew away from Anthony and looked up at him through tear-soaked lashes. "Aunt Sara?" she said in a horrified whisper. "Anthony, Aunt Sara . . ."

Anthony smiled reluctantly. "Yes. I am well aware of what your Aunt Sara does for a living," he said. "But, Rochelle, she is the only living relative within driving distance. You have no choice but to go and stay with her until . . . other arrangements are made. It's damn evident that you can't stay here."

"There's your ranch," Rochelle said, wiping a stray tear from her cheek. "I could stay there, at least until we have the . . . inn . . . repaired."

He locked his fingers onto her shoulders. He looked

sternly down at her. "I don't want to hear any more talk of returning here," he said flatly. "The inn has not only been ransacked, but nearly destroyed. It will never be the same again, Rochelle."

"Then I must stay with you, Anthony," she said, her eyes wide and pleading. "I thought that was what you would want. You are now my guardian. Why must I stay with Aunt Sara?" She had many reasons for wanting to stay with him at his ranch, but she could not disclose them to him. To be able to live the rough and wild life of Montana, she would have to learn to ride a horse, shoot a gun, and rope steers. Though Anthony's ranch was a small one with only a few cows, she knew that the practice that she would need to set her plans in motion would have to be done there.

Anthony dropped his hands to his sides and turned his head away from her. "Rochelle, I may be your guardian, but I am no kin of yours," he said thickly. "If I took you to my house, there could be talk . . . ugly talk. You are a young lady . . . I am an unwed man."

The color rose in Rochelle's cheeks. "Anthony," she gasped. "What are you saying?"

He turned his face back to her. "My child, though you and I know that our friendship would be innocent enough, it could be made to look different in the eyes of busybodies. You can't stay at my ranch without another member of your family. Please understand."

"But there is only . . . Aunt Sara. . . ." she said, her eyes again awash in tears.

"Yes. Only Aunt Sara," Anthony said, kneading his chin. "Perhaps, just perhaps—"

"Perhaps what?" Rochelle asked, tilting her head, looking up at him. She brushed her onslaught of tears away, and coughed into a hand.

"If your Aunt Sara could give up her establishment and agree to live with us at the ranch, then we could live there without the gossip-mongers interfering," Anthony said, almost beneath his breath.

Hope swelled within Rochelle. She was even able to manage a soft smile. "Do you think she would?" she said in a rush of words.

"You know your aunt; I don't," Anthony shrugged. "What do you think?"

"You've never met Aunt Sara?" Rochelle gasped. "You've known my family all these years and you've yet to meet my colorful aunt?"

Anthony chuckled. "Can't say that I've had the need to," he said. "And she hasn't made herself visible here at the inn, would you say?"

"No," Rochelle giggled. "Though she was Father's sister, I can't say that Father approved of her chosen profession. She stayed pretty much to herself at her house, with her . . . her clients."

"I can understand your father's way of thinking," Anthony chuckled. "I question also her choice of clients."

"Because of her profession I wonder if your decision to include her in my life is a wise one," Rochelle said, wrinkling her nose as she wiped it with the back of a hand. "What would Father think?"

"Your father would think first of you and only later of Sara and her profession," Anthony said dryly. "My dear, you are in need of a place to stay. Your Aunt Sara is the first to come to mind. Now let's just keep our fingers crossed that you won't have to stay at her place and that she will agree to come and stay at the ranch."

Rochelle's shoulders slumped. "She won't," she sighed. "Why would she? Her life has been quite full without me to fool with."

"She's family, isn't she?" Anthony argued.

"Well, yes. . . ."

"Well, then, that says it all," he said, nodding. "Families should and most *do* stick together. That's just the way it is . . . sort of the code of law from the beginning of time."

Rochelle gave Anthony a pinched, doubtful look, then let him sweep her into his arms to give her a big, warm, comforting bear hug.

"Things'll be all right," he murmured. "You'll see."

Two of Rochelle's trunks were filled and in the carriage, and the Jackson House Inn had been left to ruin. Rochelle sat glumly beside Anthony in the carriage as the horse traveled up a winding gravel drive, the quiet blues of the Potomac River on one side, a wide stretch of green lawn on the other.

"I much prefer going to your ranch, to live only with you," Rochelle pouted. "What is Aunt Sara to think when we just walk in on her and make the announcement that I have been orphaned and that she has been chosen to look after me in your absence?"

"It matters not what she thinks or says, she will help you, by God, or I will be the one to tell the authorities a thing or two about her clientele," Anthony responded. "Your father told me that up to now she has paid dearly to be sure to keep her house open to customers. But if enough stink is raised, no amount of money paid will ensure her opened doors."

Rochelle shivered involuntarily. "I wonder just how many women she keeps in her employ," she dared to say, still having not said the word "brothel" aloud.

Anthony knitted his heavy brows and cast Rochelle a troubled glance. "That is no concern of yours," he growled. "Just you keep your eyes from wandering once we enter that house. Your father brought you to Alexandria for an education . . . but not that kind."

"Yet you take me there, to possibly leave me, to live in the house with all those questionable goings-on?" Rochelle said disconsolately. "Anthony, I find all of this a bit hard to understand."

"As I said, we'll work something out," Anthony grumbled.

The hot red sun had emerged, making a rosy red track across the Potomac River. Sitting splendidly high on a hill straight ahead of the moving carriage stood a Victorian Gothic house, its structure dating from somewhere between early and late Victorian.

Rochelle became lost in its grandeur, having never been brought here before; her father had been so disapproving of his sister that they'd never visited.

The house was a two-story structure of gray limestone boasting door frames of golden stone. Deep, double gingerbread designs adorned the porches, and the roof was of copper. Roses bloomed in profusion in Rochelle's aunt's formal gardens, and weeping willows graced the winding walks that led from the house down to the river.

"I must say . . . she knows how to live," Anthony chuckled, also appraising everything. Then he cleared his throat nervously and gave Rochelle a quick, embarrassed look. "I must reword that," he said thickly. "Your aunt has good taste in houses and gardens."

Rochelle giggled, understanding the awkward position in which Anthony found himself. Yet it amazed her that he wasn't more a man of the world.

Anthony drew the carriage up to the carriage block and secured the horse, then went around and helped Rochelle down. He gave her a lingering look, seeing the flush of her cheeks and the wariness in her eyes.

"Are you going to be all right?" he softly asked.

She cast him a rueful glance. "My world has been suddenly torn apart and you can ask that, Anthony?" she accused.

She glanced toward the house, then back at him. "And Aunt Sara?" she whispered. "Me and Aunt Sara? I'm not so sure, Anthony."

"If your Aunt Sara has anything at all of your father in her, she will take to you quite quickly," Anthony tried to reassure her. He placed an arm about her waist. "Come on. We won't know until we see, right?"

Rochelle held back, refusing to take that first step upward. Her hands went to her bonnet, seeing that it was in its proper place, loving the feel of satin trim at its edges and the velvet ribbon tied beneath.

"Do I look all right?" she asked eagerly, letting her gaze move downward, seeing the fully-gathered cotton dress with its preponderance of lace at its high throat and at the cuff of the sleeves. Many layers of lace petticoats held the dress out away from her legs, and the tiny yellow rosebuds which dotted the white fabric seemed to come alive when the wind caught at the hem.

"Your cheeks were never rosier, nor your eyes as bright," Anthony said, wishing the latter were true. In her eyes he saw too much sadness . . . too much confusion. And this thing that he was about to do . . . was it right? But he knew that he had no other choice but to approach Sara. It just wouldn't be proper for him to take full charge of Rochelle's life.

"Then what are we waiting for?" Rochelle sighed. "We must do our best to convince Sara to leave this place and go to your ranch with us. We must!"

"We will try our damnedest!" Anthony grumbled.

Again he placed his arm possessively about her

waist, oh, loving her so much and wanting only the best for her. Even if it meant leaving her with Sara at this place of ill repute, he could see to it that Rochelle would spend most of her time at the ranch. It would just be bedtime that would concern him: she would have to sleep in Sara's establishment . . . and night was when there was the most activity there.

He had doubted all along that Sara would agree to leave her fancy house, but he hadn't wanted to trouble Rochelle with such doubts. He also knew that he couldn't draw undue attention to Sara for any legal reason, because Rochelle already lived under the stigma of her brother's questionable, untimely death. She didn't need anymore wrongful attention drawn her way. Yes, Richard was possibly a hero as far as the Confederacy was concerned, but to the Union, he was damned. . . .

Stepping up on the porch, Rochelle swallowed hard, not knowing what to expect. She had been only five the last time she had seen her Aunt Sara. She knew that her aunt wouldn't even recognize her, let alone be eager to let her become a part of her household. Rochelle didn't even want to be a part of it—but she had to stop rebelling, for Anthony's sake. Anthony's life was already enough of a turmoil because of her.

Anthony stepped up to the huge oak door, lifted the brass knocker, and let it bang noisily with three knocks. Then he stepped back, trying to give Rochelle a smile of reassurance.

She smiled weakly back at him, then jumped with a start when the door opened in a jerk to disclose a white-capped negro maid. Her face was leathery and lined with age, yet there was a dignity in her straight bearing, and her dark eyes displayed an intense warmth.

"Yes?" the maid asked, smoothing down the white apron worn over a floor-length black dress. "What may

I do for you?" Her dark eyes traveled questionably from Anthony to Rochelle and back again.

"I've come to see Sara Jackson," Anthony said, clearing his throat nervously, for beautifully dressed women were lounging around just inside the door. They sat on chairs in the sun as it rippled through the many windows in what appeared to be quite a spacious parlor.

"And who should I say is askin'?" the maid queried, eyeing Anthony, closely scrutinizing him, as she did most men who showed their face for the first time at her Sara's establishment. "Do you have an appointment, suh?"

Anthony lifted a finger to the tightness of his stiffly starched white collar, feeling itchy from perspiration. "No. No appointment," he said thickly. "I've come to see Miss Jackson about her niece, Rochelle. Maybe she hasn't heard . . . but there have been two recent deaths in the family."

"Yassuh. She knows. She received word. She just couldn't bear to go to the funerals," the maid apologized. "My baby Sara . . . she ain't so strong at times."

Anthony looked at Rochelle questioningly. "Did you send word to your Aunt Sara about your father and brother?" he said softly.

Rochelle lowered her eyes. "Yes. I did," she murmured.

"And she didn't bother to come to the funerals?" he growled.

Rochelle let her eyes slowly drift upward. "No. That's another reason I didn't think coming here was such a good idea," she said.

"Why didn't you tell me that you had contacted her and she had refused to at least pay her last respects to her brother and nephew?" he snapped. "What kind of person is she?"

"Oh? And you are ready to judge me, sir, without first meeting me?" A voice soft and silky as honey came suddenly from the doorway.

Anthony's head jerked around. His mouth dropped open when he saw the vision before him. She was not at all as he had imagined her. In such a profession, he would have thought to have found someone hard . . . crass . . . even aged for one of thirty years.

But instead, she was all soft-looking, lovely, yet not petite like her niece Rochelle. She was fleshy in all the right places, her breasts her best commodity as they now almost spilled from the bodice of her fancy silk dress.

Anthony couldn't help but stare. She was of middle height, her complexion as pure as alabaster, and she had a pair of dangerous-looking hazel eyes, with a Roman nose and a small and prettily formed mouth.

Her auburn hair was neatly banded and gathered in a tasteful, ornamented net with a roll and gold tassels at the side. How sedate she looked in her scarlet dress with its broad black trim at the skirt and sleeves, a diamond necklace at her plunging neckline, matching earrings at her graceful earlobes.

"Sir, has the cat got your tongue?" Sara asked, laughing silkily. Then she let her gaze move to Rochelle. "And Rochelle, don't you have a hug for your Aunt Sara? Or did your father turn you completely against me?"

Rochelle lifted her chin proudly. "Father never said much about you one way or the other," she said, trying not to show any overt disrespect to her aunt because of her chosen profession.

"I'm so sorry about Daniel and Richard," Sara said,

moving around her maid, out onto the porch, to tenderly hug Rochelle. "I just couldn't come, Rochelle. Please understand?"

Rochelle stiffened in Sara's embrace. "It was not a pleasant thing to have to attend," she murmured. "Yes. Of course I will try to understand."

She squirmed out of her aunt's arms. "So you do recognize me?" she asked shyly. "It's been so long, Aunt Sara. It's as though we lived across the world from one another, instead of just across the city of Alexandria."

"Of course I would recognize my very own niece," Sara said, all bubbly. "And I apologize for not having come to see you all these years. But Daniel wanted it that way. He, well, he didn't approve of many things that I do."

"Yes. I knew at least that much," Rochelle replied.

Sara gave Anthony an interesting stare, then slowly looked him up and down. She liked what she saw, his rugged handsomeness. She tilted her head sideways in a flirtatious look that she had grown accustomed to using on men that fascinated her.

"And your name, sir?" Sara asked, offering him a hand.

"Anthony. Anthony Oliver," he said in a deep, resonant voice. He took her hand in his and the touch, so much like that of rose petals, sent his heart to racing. She was captivating him and he did not want this. A woman like her could never be right for him. He wanted a great deal in a wife, perhaps *too* much, for he had yet to find one to share his name!

Sara solidly grasped Anthony's hand, seeing in his eyes that she had won him over without having even tried. "And why are you here with my niece, Anthony?" she asked, giving Rochelle another soft smile.

"Rochelle needs family at this time in her life," Anthony said dryly. "Sara, you are the only one who is available. You must agree to aid Rochelle since she has nobody else."

Sara blanched. She drew her hand quickly away from Anthony, gasping. "Lord!" she blurted. "What did you say?"

"Let's at least talk about it," Anthony encouraged. "Perhaps we could step into your parlor, and discuss Rochelle's future."

"Rochelle cannot stay here," Sara said stiffly, her smile having deserted her. "It's as simple as that."

"I didn't come to ask that Rochelle stay here," Anthony said. "I am about to ask that you move to my ranch, to live with Rochelle and me, so that it will be all right that Rochelle live under my roof. With you there, it would look respectable. No one would accuse me of taking advantage of two women."

Sara placed a hand to her brow. "My word, but you do have an imagination," she laughed. "I wouldn't live on a ranch . . . I wouldn't live anywhere with you. Not for Rochelle. Not for anything nor anybody. And as for looking respectable? Surely you jest when speaking of how people feel about me. Respectable is an adjective far removed from me, Anthony, as far as most people are concerned."

"We must at least talk about it," Anthony grumbled. "She is your kin. You can't turn your back on her, Sara."

Sara's eyes softened as she looked Rochelle up and down. Then she gave Anthony a harried glance. "Oh, all right," she said. "Come on in. At least we can talk. But don't expect anything of me. I have my own life. I don't need the likes of you, sir, to try and change anything about it."

"Talk is all I came for now," he said, smiling coyly down at her. "Now how about it?"

Sara stepped aside. Rochelle followed alongside Anthony into a house of grand proportions. The ceilings were high, giving the house a feeling of great spaciousness; a wide marble stairway reached to the second floor; and ornately framed mirrors, big enough to reflect a crowd, looked back onto the parlor that they had just entered.

The parlor was filled with priceless furniture. It was apparent that Sara reveled in the beauty of her house. Deep, comfortable, thick-cushioned chairs and sofas, upholstered in subtle shades of brown and pink, were set to provide a sweeping view of the Potomac. The golden wood floors were bare, the walls and ceilings white. The windows were wide and the shutters had been thrown open to the welcome splash of the sun.

On the far wall, opposite the windows, a masterful stone fireplace was surrounded by various and sundry chairs and tables. There was a magnificent chandelier of brass and crystal hanging over a long oak table which displayed crystal goblets and tall-stemmed glasses to match.

As Rochelle was led into the far reaches of the parlor, she now began quizzically looking at the lounging women, all dressed in expensive gowns with shining jewelry at their exposed white throats and long fingers.

Blushing, knowing what these women did for a living, she turned her eyes away and welcomed a chair which faced the river view and not the women.

"Will this do?" Sara asked, making a sweeping gesture toward three chairs arranged closely together.

"Fine," Anthony said, nodding toward Rochelle.

"Wine? Or cake and coffee?" Sara asked, folding her hands together.

"Nothing, thanks," Rochelle politely answered, placing her hands on her lap.

"Nor for me," Anthony said, settling down into a chair beside Rochelle.

Sara slipped easily into a chair beside Anthony and looked solicitously over at him. "And now, what did you want us to talk about?" she murmured.

"Rochelle . . . you must help Rochelle until we can think of something better," Anthony said, patting his knee nervously.

Sara laughed. "I do not take that as a compliment, sir," she said. "Until Rochelle finds something better? Better than me? Is that what you implied?"

Anthony leaned forward. "My name is Anthony," he said dryly. "And I didn't mean to imply anything of the kind, though you must know that this would not be the best environment for your niece."

"Then why did you bring her here?" Sara asked, sighing heavily.

"I did not come here to play games," Anthony growled. "You know why we're here. Now will you agree to help us, or not?"

Sara shook her head and again sighed. "What on earth do you expect me to do?" she asked. "Rochelle surely doesn't want to stay here."

"I said before what I thought would be best for her," Anthony said, his jaw hard. "Come out to my ranch. Stay there. Let her live where she will be free to come and go, to commune with nature."

Sara rose hastily to her feet. She glared down at Anthony. "If that is all you have to say, you might as well leave," she snapped. "I will not leave my house. I have already told you that."

Anthony rose to his feet and challenged Sara with a

set stare, his hands on his hips. "Then she must stay here, for at least a while," he said angrily.

Sara stood on tiptoe, glaring into his face. "Just who are you to say what she does or does not do?" she hissed. "And you certainly have no right to come into my home and tell me or Rochelle what to do!"

"I was Daniel's best friend," he told her. "We've been together since our mavericking days in Texas. I have been appointed Rochelle's guardian. I must see that she is well taken care of."

"If you are her guardian, take her with you," Sara insisted.

"I told you, I cannot do that," Anthony repeated.

Rochelle rose to her feet, tears streaming down her face. She glowered first at Sara and then at Anthony. "Will you quit discussing me as though I'm not even here?" she shouted. "I'm sorry I'm so much bother! I'm sorry I didn't die along with Father and Richard!"

She hung her head and began to run toward the door, blinded by her tears. She jerked when she felt a hand on each of her arms. Anthony was at her right side, Sara at her left.

"Let me go. . . ." she cried.

"I'm sorry, Rochelle," Sara said, letting her hand slip into Rochelle's.

"Rochelle, damn it, I'm sorry," Anthony said, his hand slipping about her waist.

"I don't need either of you," she sobbed. "I can make my own way in the world . . . you'll see."

"That won't be necessary," Sara said, giving Anthony a sour glance across Rochelle's shoulder. "Between Anthony and me, we'll see to your welfare. I'm sorry I made such a fuss over it. You can stay here as long as you wish."

Anthony gave Sara a frown. "You would do better at the ranch," he grumbled.

"I know that you think that," Sara argued. "But believe me, Anthony, things aren't as bad here as you would think for the raising of a young lady. My maid Priscilla has a daughter Rochelle's age. She has her quarters here in the house and she hasn't been tainted by the gentlemen callers at all. My clientele are only the best . . . gentlemen—in every sense of the word. What goes on here goes on behind closed doors."

"Then she will stay," Anthony said. He placed a forefinger beneath Rochelle's chin and lifted her face so that he would see deep into her eyes. "Honey, it's the only way. I'm sorry . . . sorry as hell."

"I'll be all right," she whispered, then threw herself against Anthony and again took comfort from his warm embrace.

Four

Four years later

The war was over. Rochelle had patiently waited, all the while learning the skills of riding, roping steers, and shooting a pistol, as she had planned. But now was the time to proceed with her plans.

As she had hoped, it had been easy enough to follow the military career of Steven Browning. If the newspapers weren't hailing his heroism, the ladies of Washington were. Steven had been promoted to the rank of Colonel and had even been seen occasionally on a fine steed on his way to visit the President at the White House. And now that the war was over, Rochelle knew to expect him back in Washington.

She had readied herself for this . . . with a plan to meet him, to find out what his future plans were. She hoped they still included the territory of Montana. She had been talking about Montana to Anthony, spurring his interest in moving there. Her only fear had been that he might want to make the move before Rochelle had had a chance to meet Steven Browning face-to-face, to see just where he planned to settle. Only by knowing this could she proceed with her vengeance. . . .

For now, she had secretly taken a room at an elegant hotel close to the Capitol building, giving her the full view of it. If Steven were to arrive back in town, she would surely see him, even if she managed to position herself in the hotel room several times each day, trying to keep Anthony from finding out what she was up to.

But at present she was galloping across the meadow on a magnificent chestnut steed with Anthony riding beside her. This was the time of day that she always waited for . . . when she was free, riding against the wind, with Anthony as her companion. They had grown close . . . closer even than Rochelle had been to her brother Richard. Guilt had sometimes plagued her when she realized this, yet it warmed her heart to know that she had someone she could fully depend on, forever, if necessary, as long as she showed that she needed him.

The sun was hot on her face, unusually hot for the month of April, but Rochelle basked in it. It had been a long, cold winter, filled with the torment of war throughout the state of Virginia. It had even been said that Virginia had been most adversely affected by the war and that some cities now stood in ruins.

Not having traveled while war was raging, Rochelle hadn't witnessed any of this tragedy firsthand. She had been protected not only by Anthony, but also by her Aunt Sara, who had become more loving toward her.

It hadn't even been a problem for Rochelle to live at her Aunt Sara's "house." Rochelle had been given quarters on the second floor, with her own private parlor, bedroom, and library. Rochelle had never been approached by any of the men who sought pleasure from Aunt Sara's beautiful women. . . .

Anthony rode closer to Rochelle, wondering about

the energy that she seemed never to use up. It was as though she was driven by some unseen force.

Of late, this appeared to have strengthened. She now worked incessantly with the pistol and urged him to teach her more and more about roping steers. Her interest in Montana had even become more evident. But perhaps her need to move elsewhere stemmed from the fact that war had left everything in Virginia so ugly . . . so undesirable for such a young, beautiful woman.

Anthony silently studied Rochelle. She wore jeans, a plaid cotton shirt, and a Stetson which only partially hid the red flame of her hair. The past years had witnessed her maturing into a lovely woman. Now twenty, her face had lost all traces of its childish freckles and had turned a milky white touched by pale pinks, now even rosy beneath the tinting rays of the sun.

Everything about her face was beautiful—the wide, green eyes, heavily lashed; the tiny nose; the sweet lips. Her exquisite, slim neck led one's eyes downward, where she had blossomed out magnificently. Her breasts even now swelled prettily, straining against the cotton of her shirt.

She was a woman . . . a desirous woman . . . there was no doubting that. One day there would be a man in her life. Anthony only hoped he would approve. He wanted only the best for his Rochelle! And, ah, wasn't she vulnerable in her loveliness . . . ?

"Isn't it just too beautiful a day, Anthony?" Rochelle asked him across her shoulder as she raced faster.

Anthony laughed to himself and pressed his knees into his horse. His dark hair flying, he drew rein beside her. "Wait up," he said. "Where's the fire, Rochelle?"

Rochelle tightened the reins and drew her steed to a shivering halt. She looked over at Anthony, smiling wickedly. "What's the matter?" she teased. "Can't your horse keep up? Anthony, if we're going to move to Montana, you'd best be sure to get yourself a more-spirited steed."

Anthony frowned. There was the mention of Montana again. She certainly seemed determined to throw it into the conversation lately. He now knew that she was serious about the move, though he should have known long ago that she was. He had never seen anyone so determined to learn the ways of the West. And she had been an obedient student. She could now be a part of the Montana life and survive it well.

Giving Rochelle a playful look, he reached and took her reins. "Montana, is it?" he chuckled. "So you again speak of Montana?"

She looked over at him, seeing the soft smile lighting his face. In his jeans, cowboy boots, and fancy embroidered cotton shirt, he did look like a cowboy, a man of the West. His face was already tanned; it had been a warm spring.

"Don't you feel it, Anthony?" she said, now looking about her at the budding trees, the green stretch of meadow dotted by early wildflowers of yellow and blue. The sky was a brilliant blue, with only an occasional wisp of clouds skipping along the horizon. The Potomac glistened in the sun.

Anthony followed her gaze. He leaned over his saddle horn. "Feel what?" he queried.

Gesturing with a full sweep of her hand, Rochelle again let her eyes take in the beauty of the day, inhaling the fresh air that blew in from the river. "The beauty of the countryside," Rochelle shouted. "It makes me feel so alive . . . so vibrant. Just think how it must be in Montana, where everything is untouched . . . so wild and untamed."

Her shadowed eyes moved to Anthony, where she

saw an added look of amusement raising his lips into an almost teasing smile. "Anthony, why are you looking at me like that?" she asked. "What is it you haven't told me?"

Anthony relaxed in his saddle, returning her reins to her. "It's this interest you have in Montana," he said, swinging out of his saddle. He went to Rochelle and helped her from her horse. "What would you say if I told you that I've sent an associate of mine to Montana to find us a favorable spread of land?"

Rochelle took a step away from Anthony, her face pinched in a sudden frown. "You've done what?" she gasped.

Anthony's smile faded when he saw her immediate displeasure. "Why do I get the feeling that you don't approve? Rochelle, I thought it was *you* who wanted to go to Montana. You know I left my wanderlust far behind me long ago. I've only decided to consider Montana because of you. Isn't this what you want?"

Rochelle lowered her eyes. She went to Anthony and embraced him. "You're too good to me," she sighed. "I'm sorry if I acted so . . . so spoiled. Yes, of course I want to go to Montana." But she couldn't tell him that she didn't want to determine just *where* in Montana until she found out where Steven Browning planned to settle down. Montana was a vast territory, and Rochelle and Steven could be separated by miles. Somehow she had to make sure this didn't happen.

"Then you do still want to go to Montana?" Anthony asked thickly.

Rochelle eased away from him. "The adventure would interest me," she said softly, not wanting to act too eager. She needed time, but how could she tell him that? He was never to know what she carried in her heart. He would never approve of what she'd planned.

He was a man who hardly knew the meaning of the word "hate."

"Adventure?" he asked, incredulous, chuckling. "Is that what you'd call it? Uprooting ourselves to leave the only way of life that you have ever known? I would call it lunacy. You do know that in Montana there are more Indians than white men, don't you?"

Rochelle pushed back the brim of her hat and wiped away a bead of perspiration. "The thought of Indians does not frighten me," she shrugged. "And as far as uprooting myself, I can't see how leaving Aunt Sara's could be anything but good for me."

"Has it been all that unbearable?" Anthony had become attached to Sara in ways Rochelle was not aware of. Though he'd found Sara's way of life distasteful, he had found *her* alluring. With Sara, there was a wildness shared. Even sparks of love had been kindled.

Rochelle tossed her head. "Not unbearable," she said softly. She swung herself back up into her saddle. "But I would prefer something much different now, Anthony. I'm not getting any younger. I feel that if I don't get away from that house and those men I will be stifled for life. I want to live . . . fully live. I want to feel free, free to do as I please . . . whenever I please. At Aunt Sara's I have to stay too much to myself."

Anthony walked away from her, his heart heavy that he had not been able to do any better for her. "We will go to Montana as soon as I find a suitable place to build my ranch," he said flatly.

Again Rochelle flinched; she felt trapped. He seemed *too* anxious to go, and it was *time* that she needed.

Frustration swam inside her. "Anthony, just where do you think you . . . uh . . . might settle in Montana?" she dared to ask. "Or do you even have any idea?"

"I've sent my associate to the Fort Benton area," he

said matter-of-factly. "It's a bridgehead between steamer and wagon trains. If we can settle near there, I think we'd do all right."

"Fort Benton. . . ." Rochelle murmured, knowing she must remember that. When she contacted Steven Browning, she must somehow bring up that name in conversation.

Rochelle was now full of doubts, thinking that nothing would ever work out for her. Perhaps she had only been fooling herself all these years in thinking that she would ever again even see Steven Browning. But it had kept her going, this need. . . .

Redolent of perfume, Rochelle's freshly washed hair glistened. She now stood brushing it before a mirror, dressed in a loose and flowing silk robe, ready for bed. Out of the corner of her eye she caught the movement of Jolene, her young Negro maid, readying her bed. Rochelle could see Jolene glancing at the photograph of Steven on the end table. Rochelle had only recently taken the photograph from its hiding place to begin studying it again. She had to believe he would return to Washington to meet with President Lincoln before going on with his life, now that the war was over.

It had been a while since she had seen him, but she just couldn't let herself think that anything might have happened to him, even though many hadn't made it through the war alive.

"I just have to ask," Jolene said, stopping to pick up the photograph to study it more closely. "Who is this here man? I ain't never seen him before. Why, you never see no men. Why do you have a photograph of one here beside your bed?"

Rochelle spun around; her face flushed with color.

"Oh, that," she said, taking another long stroke with her brush through her hair. "That's only something I picked up in the city. It's sort of a souvenir photograph they are selling. I . . . uh . . . kind of liked the way it looked. That's all."

Jolene's dark eyes widened and her teeth flashed in a teasing smile. "Now that makes no sense," she giggled. "Why'd you buy anything that didn't mean beans to you? Is this here a photograph of someone you know, even like? You're not the kind to waste money on trivials."

In three wide strides, silk flying, Rochelle grabbed the photograph from Jolene's clutches. She frowned at her maid. "It isn't any of your business," she snapped. "Just because you're my best friend doesn't mean I'm going to tell you everything about what I think or do."

Jolene shrugged and continued making up Rochelle's bed. "Don't matter none if you don't tell me," she giggled. She cast Rochelle a coy look over her shoulder. "But does it have anythin' to do with that room you've taken in Washington?"

Rochelle slipped the photograph beneath her mattress. "I thought it didn't matter whether I told you or not," she softly laughed.

"I was speakin' of that photograph," Jolene said, stopping to place her hands to the small of her back as she stretched. Though only nineteen, she had all the aches and pains of an old woman, and she had begun to worry about whether or not she would be able to make the trip to Montana with Rochelle, though such talk had been a secret between them. It seemed to Jolene that she had inherited her mama's aches and pains; her mama was Sara's maid and confidante, just as Jolene was for Rochelle.

"Just hush about the photograph and the room," Rochelle said, yawning. She tossed her brush aside and slipped between the cool sheets. "I don't want Sara or Anthony to know about them, either, do you hear, Jolene?"

"Yas'm," Jolene giggled. "Whatever my misses says. I don't want to hamper your plans, whatever they are." She gave Rochelle a pleading look. "Rochelle, tell me," she encouraged. "I won't tell a soul. Honest."

Rochelle leaned up on an elbow and looked at Jolene, seeing her tininess, her lovely face, and the frilly, lace-trimmed, white cotton dress which made her dark skin look almost blue.

In the past four years, Jolene had become her best friend; they usually confided to each other everything that happened. Since Jolene was the daughter of Priscilla, Sara's personal maid, it was easy for Rochelle to become close to her. They usually spent most evening hours together, sharing dreams and talking of future plans and hopes.

Rochelle had always known that Jolene's future depended on her and the responsibility made her heart heavy at times. Though born with the idea that slavery was the way of the world, she had never liked the idea of having a maid.

So she'd chosen to make Jolene more than just a maid. And when the day came to travel to Montana, Jolene would be there sharing in the adventure.

Rochelle reached up and touched Jolene's satin cheek. She smiled warmly at her. "Later," she said, "I promise to tell you later. But I can't now. I'm not even sure myself how to do what needs to be done."

"Needs to be done?" Jolene asked, curling her lips.

"Jolene, just trust me," Rochelle said, now easing back down onto her fluffed pillow. "I will tell you everything, once I know it myself."

Jolene placed a hand to her back and groaned as she straightened herself to a standing position. "All right," she sighed.

"Is your back hurting again?" Rochelle asked, frowning.

"Just like my mama's misery," Jolene said. "It ain't nothin'. It always passes." She giggled. "Sometimes I feel like an old lady."

"Rheumatism gets worse in the spring, when it's damp from the rain," Rochelle murmured. "You'll feel better when we get to Montana."

Jolene's eyes brightened and her soreness was quickly forgotten. She flopped down on the bed and kicked her shoes off, slipping her feet beneath her. "Tell me all about it again," she said anxiously. "It sure do sound like a different world."

"I don't know that much about it, Jolene," Rochelle laughed. "I just know what I've read in books at the library."

"Are there Indians?"

"Yes . . . many."

Jolene shuddered visibly. Her hands went to the tight black curls which circled her tiny head. "Do you think we will get scalped?"

Rochelle giggled. "If I thought that, I wouldn't think of going," she said.

A light tap on the door drew Jolene from the bed. Barefoot, she answered the knock, finding Sara there, beautiful in a green satin dress with a plunging neckline. Her auburn hair was in a lovely swirl atop her head and diamonds sparkled at her throat, earlobes, and on several fingers.

"Yas'm?" Jolene asked, taking a step backward as Sara entered the bedroom.

Sara smiled politely at Jolene and then walked on

over to settle down on the edge of the bed. Her long, tapered fingers went to Rochelle's hair and smoothed it back from her ears. "Darlin', I've some news that has just been brought by one of my men callers."

Rochelle sat up, the silk of her gown rustling against the silk sheet. "What is it, Aunt Sara?" she asked, seeing something distant in her aunt's usually vibrant eyes.

"It's President Lincoln," Sara said slowly. "He's been shot. He's not expected to last the night."

Rochelle's mouth dropped open; she was speechless. She couldn't help but remember that day many years ago when she had stood in the same room as President Lincoln and witnessed his gentleness. From then on she'd never been able to think ill of him though he was, in a sense, responsible for her brother's and father's deaths.

It was hard to believe that such a man could be dying . . . that his life could be snuffed out after so many years of turmoil and hardship. The thought of his strikingly beautiful gray eyes, once so full of tenderness and kindness, now about to be stilled by death was incomprehensible.

"Who could do such a thing?" she blurted.

"I don't know," Sara said, rising to her feet. "I just thought you might want to know. Everyone has left the house for the night. They're all in a state of shock."

"Yes . . . I'm sure," Rochelle whispered. She couldn't help but think about what this turn of events could mean to her and her plans. If President Lincoln died, wouldn't all important military personnel be dispatched to Washington for the funeral?

Remembering another such ceremony, Rochelle now understood what she must do. Again she would dress in black. Again she would sort through the crowd for a pair of piercing blue eyes. . . .

* * *

Rochelle stood in the East Room of the White House, feeling as though time had turned back four years. It seemed to her that she saw the same people now as she had at Colonel Elmer Ellsworth's funeral. The only difference was the burial: a great train awaited the arrival of Lincoln's body to carry it slowly from Washington to Springfield, Illinois.

A black veil shielding her face from view, Rochelle mingled among the crowd of dignitaries, keeping her eyes alert for Steven Browning. But so far all uniforms seemed to look the same; all faces were solemn, stricken quiet with remorse.

Lifting the skirts of her black dress, Rochelle made a quiet sweep about the room, stopping when she saw something familiar about a man who was bent over, speaking quietly to a lady, his back to Rochelle.

A dull ache knotted within Rochelle's chest at the sound of his familiar, gentle drawl. She recognized his powerful back, shoulders, and legs; his hair was even more yellow than she remembered, combed neatly to lie just above his collar line. His uniform was impeccably pressed, its navy blue color a dreadful reminder of whose side he fought so valiantly for in the war.

When he straightened up and turned to scan the room, Rochelle's breath was taken from her as she encountered the familiar piercing blue of his eyes.

Finally, after all these years, she was being given the opportunity to meet Steven Browning again. She was glad he hadn't perished at the hands of the Confederacy during the war. She wasn't sure if she was glad because she was to get her vengeance, or because she was going to get to talk to him again.

She didn't want to believe the latter . . . but there

was no denying that she had spent many nights thinking of him and his many charms. She almost hated the fact that she had ever begun including him in her thoughts.

Something akin to passion flooded Rochelle's senses when he looked directly her way. Having fought in the war had put more muscle on him, and now that she was being afforded a closer look, she saw that he had grayed somewhat at the temples.

And then her heart skipped a beat; she saw a minute scar above his left eyebrow where she skin seemed to pucker and draw his eyebrow up just slightly. She now knew that he hadn't been entirely spared of wounds in battle. She couldn't help but whisper a small prayer of thanks that the wound was small, that he had been spared greater suffering.

Now it was time to proceed with her plan; she longed to get on with her life, a life which would, she hoped, include Steven Browning. With a pounding heart and weak knees, she made her way toward Lincoln's casket. She tried not to worry about whether Steven would have to come to her rescue if she began showing signs of fainting, or whether or not he would even recognize her if, indeed, he did help guide her from the room. All that she could do was give it a wholehearted try, having thought of hardly anything else but him the past four years.

Feeling his eyes follow her to the casket, Rochelle was strangely lightheaded just knowing that he was there, that his eyes were on her. Oh, how long had she waited for this moment! She couldn't let herself weaken now and run from the room as her heart was begging her to do. She had waited too long to fail now!

Sweeping around the full tail of her dress, she stepped up to the casket and peered down at the still face of Abraham Lincoln. Something gripped her insides as she saw the gentleness this man's face radiated. Tears burned at the corners of her eyes when she saw the bold firmness of his nose, his pronounced, granite chin, and his heavy lower lip. His eyes were peacefully closed; no longer could one see their penetrating tenderness.

A sudden shame engulfed Rochelle; she felt as though she had used President Lincoln for her own devious purposes. How could she have thought to use this moment, a time of grieving over the President, for her own gainful purposes?

Tears fell profusely down her face; she emitted a loud sob as she lowered her face into her hands. And when a powerful arm encircled her waist and began guiding her from the room, she was glad. She didn't even care that it wasn't Steven Browning. All she wanted was to get away, far away from this place where she had shamed herself.

"We all feel the same," a voice said in a low, gentle drawl. "Just cry it all out. Then you'll feel better, ma'am."

Rochelle's heart lurched as she heard the familiar voice: it was Steven Browning after all who so gallantly escorted her from the room. She didn't dare look up at him. Though she wore a black veil, she was afraid that he could see clean into her soul and know her every thought. Steven Browning: he was here with her, every handsome inch of him, and she didn't like the way he was making her feel. She wanted to hate him, not be infatuated by him!

She kept her head slightly bowed, and dabbed her nose with her handkerchief. "I thank you, sir," she murmured. "You are very kind. I became so . . . so distraught. I do appreciate you rescuing me."

"Are you in the company of a husband, or some

other relative who should be with you, look after you?" Steven asked, guiding her down a spacious corridor.

"No; no one," Rochelle said. "I have come to the city for only this one day and night, to pay my respects to the President."

"That is commendable," Steven said thickly. "Where are you staying? Shall I escort you there? Or do you feel well enough to return to the services?"

Rochelle's pulse began to race. He was playing right into her hands, though she had just about decided that it would be better to find another way to meet him later. But this was too good an opportunity to pass up: it was as if he'd asked to accompany her to her hotel room. Wasn't this what she'd wanted all along, having secured the room? To get him infatuated with her could solve many problems, not the least of which was learning where in Montana he was going to settle . . . if he still planned to go there. It would be ironic if he now planned to go somewhere else after she'd interested Anthony in moving to Montana.

"I do believe I should return to my hotel," she murmured. Her fingers moved toward her veil, trembling. She knew that the years had changed her. What if he did remember her? He had now seen her twice, but both times she had been a skinny teenager with a face full of freckles. Now she was twenty, and quite the lady.

Lifting the veil, she slowly turned her eyes upward to meet his watchful gaze. She looked at him carefully, watching for any signs of recognition; when she saw a trace of it, her insides splashed cold.

Steven scratched his brow idly. His eyes squinted. "Have we met before?" he asked quizzically. "There's something very familiar about your face."

"Sir, I do not know you, nor have I never seen you

before," Rochelle said softly, almost breathless with worry. "I am sure there are dozens of women who might resemble me."

Steven's eyes sparkled. He chuckled amusedly. "No; I doubt that," he said, his eyes slowly taking her in. There was much about her that made his heart thunder against his chest.

His gaze captured the sweetness of her: the demure face, etched with delicate cheekbones blooming with color; a tiny nose; perfectly formed lips; and her wide green eyes shadowed by thick lashes.

Her petiteness showed in her slender, long neck and slim waist, yet her ripe and curving bosom caused his blood to race.

In her black, lowswept cotton dress trimmed with lace, her flaming red hair flowing freely down her back, she appeared vulnerable, one surely in need of protection.

Damn it, what was there about her that was so familiar? Had their paths crossed before? The war had managed to almost block out all the good in his past. And hadn't she said that they had never met? Surely they hadn't. . . .

"It would honor me, miss, if you would permit me to escort you to your hotel, to be sure that you get there safely," Steven said, half bowing toward her, yet never taking his eyes off her.

Rochelle looked coyly aside, pretending shyness. "Sir, that isn't necessary," she murmured. "I do not need assistance; my hotel is quite near." Her heart pounded hard for fear that her self-reliance would be cause for him to leave her. Then where would she be? But she must not appear too forward. . . .

"Well, miss, I must insist," Steven said flatly, taking

her by an elbow, already walking her away from the door.

"But, sir, mustn't you return . . . ?"

"I have paid my respects. No more is required of me here."

"Then I would appreciate your continuing kindness," Rochelle said, overjoyed with the fact that so far, she had won. . . .

"But I can do so only under one condition," Steven said, stopping to take her hand. He looked down into her eyes, smiling.

Rochelle swallowed hard, now swept up in a strange rapture, something very unfamiliar to her. "And that is . . . ?" she dared to ask.

"That you first tell me your name."

Rochelle breathed easier. A smile touched her lips. "My name?" she said, her eyes sparkling. "Rochelle. Rochelle. . . ."

She paused. If she spoke the name Jackson, would he recall another Jackson? Another time? A fateful day of four years ago?

But she thought not. Jackson was a common name. "Rochelle Jackson," she blurted.

Then she tilted her head and gave him one of her most alluring smiles. "And yours, sir?" she murmured.

"Steven Browning," he chuckled. "Colonel Steven Browning at your service, ma'am."

"Colonel Browning, I am glad to make your acquaintance," Rochelle said, curtsying.

She smiled smugly to herself as he hailed a carriage. . . .

Five

Steven escorted Rochelle inside Pennsylvania House Hotel and to the staircase which led to the second floor. She turned and looked up at him, not wanting him to stop there, but not knowing how to urge him on up to her room without seeming like a whore. She knew that their time together couldn't be just that shared in a carriage between the White House and the hotel; there had to be more—much more. She had to get him to talk about his dreams . . . his future.

"Rochelle, perhaps you will agree to have dinner with me later?" Steven said, his eyes telling her that he, too, was reluctant to say farewell.

Rochelle smiled sweetly up at him. "Why, that would be nice," she said, but knew that even that was not enough. How could she get him to accompany her to her room without just asking him outright?

Then she remembered . . . though she knew it was devious, she had to try it once again. Placing her fingertips suddenly to her brow, she emitted a soft moan and swayed against Steven.

His heart lurched; his eyes widened. He placed a hand to her elbow and leaned down into her face. "Ma'am, are you feeling faint?" he gasped. "Are you still distraught from your experience at the White House?"

"I'm not sure what is the matter," she softly uttered, shaking her head, blinking her eyes as she gave him another half-glance. "Perhaps it's best if . . . I go on to my room. . . ."

"If you would accept my offer, I will escort you, Rochelle," Steven said thickly. His heart pounded at the thought of being alone with her in the privacy of a room, even if only for a moment. So much about her moved him . . . and she seemed to touch his heart. The war had been long . . . ah, such a lonely time for him. Just how long had it been since he'd had a woman?

Yet he couldn't let himself even think of that, not with this lovely lady, whose innocence was reflected in the gentle green pools of her eyes and in her quiet smile. His hungers would have to be fed elsewhere, another time. He would behave like a gentleman in this innocent's presence and hope that one day they would find themselves together. . . .

"It wouldn't be too much bother . . . too much an inconvenience?" Rochelle asked, lowering her eyes shyly. "I do not wish to be a bother; I'm sure you have someone waiting for you." Her gaze moved slowly up to his handsome face again. "Perhaps your wife is awaiting your return?" she dared to ask, not having even ventured to let herself think that he was married. If he was, so much would change!

"No . . . no bother, and no, no wife," Steven said, smiling warmly down at her. "And you?" he tested. "Is there a husband?" Damn. Why hadn't he thought that there might be? Yet there was an innocence about her . . . her radiance seemed to say that she was yet to be touched by a man. . . .

"No . . . no husband," she softly laughed. Then she

made herself remember that she was supposed to be feeling faint and again pretended a swoon. She smiled to herself when he caught her and let her lean fully against him as he began guiding her up the carpeted staircase.

The second floor landing was reached, and then the third, and then the fourth. "My room is on this floor," Rochelle softly said, her pulse racing, Steven still with her, her room so close. Dare she take the key from her purse and hand it to him? Would he follow the suggestion and unlock and open the door for her? Would he enter the room? Should she invite him in, offer him a glass of wine? Would he think poorly of her, or would he think she was afraid to be alone, in her delicate condition?

She noticed how quiet he had become as they walked down the narrow corridor which was softly lighted by candles flickering in wall sconces. She felt the tenseness in his arm as he held her about the waist. What was he thinking? What was he planning to do?

Knowing that she would have to be a bit brazen to assure that he would accompany her into the room, she eased away from him and opened her purse, reaching for the key. And then without words, only a look of utter shyness, she handed it to him.

Steven's heart pounded against his ribs. Oh, he so wanted her to desire what his loins were aching for. But he knew he might as well wish for the moon; for he was in the presence of a lady, surely one of inexperience. He would remain a gentleman, or hate himself later.

With doubt darkening his face, Steven accepted the key, inserted it into the lock, and turned it. Without looking her way, he opened the door and stepped aside so that she could enter. He watched as she glided noiselessly around to look reluctantly at him. Their eyes locked, Steven handed her the key.

As though some unseen force moved her hand, Rochelle reached upward to his face and softly touched his cheek. She had wanted to do that for so long! Her insides seemed to melt as his eyes softened and he smiled enticingly down at her. Then she forced herself to break this strange spell; she quickly grabbed the key and spun around, placing her back to him.

"Rochelle," Steven said huskily, reaching to take her hand. He spun her back around to face him. Then he lost his nerve, seeing the frightened look in her eyes. He dropped his hands to his sides. He laughed awkwardly. "I guess I'd best leave."

Panic rose inside Rochelle. She went to the door and eased it closed, then again forced herself to weave and held her face in her hand. "Please, Steven, if you could only stay for a little while longer," she murmured. "At least . . . at least until I feel stronger."

Steven frowned, puzzled, looking toward the closed door, wondering why she had closed it unless it was because she hungered for privacy.

Yet he still didn't think that she wanted anything more than talk. And how could he even think of anything so . . . so . . . obscene, when she was obviously so unwell?

Shame filled him. He went to her and let her lean against him. "Let me help you off with your wrap," he said. "Then, perhaps, you might like a glass of wine? I see that some has already been placed in your room."

Rochelle burned beneath the touch of his hand as he slipped the cape from her shoulders and the veil from her head. She was becoming more and more confused by her feelings, wanting to fight everything but the hate she should logically feel for him. But her body failed her; so much felt delicious, and all because of him.

Almost timidly she walked away from him. She closed her eyes, trying to force the death scene of her brother back into consciousness, to make her remember what must be done. These new sensual feelings surely arose only because of the moment . . . finding herself alone with a man in a hotel room . . . tempting so much to happen that was sinfully wrong. She had always wondered about the mysteries of men and women together. Surely there was pure magic to be had, and she hungered for the knowledge of such magic, yet she could not want this to happen . . . not with Steven Browning!

He walked across the room and poured two glasses of wine. Gently he handed one to Rochelle as she eased down into a chair, seeming to evade him now for some reason. Was it timidity? Was this her first time? Why was she so trusting of him? She had been the one to close the door. That was usually done only when a woman openly invited a man to her bed. But this sweet thing? No . . . it was because of her weakened state! He had to keep remembering that. He must not touch her again. . . .

Rochelle accepted it, thanking him softly, then sipped from it, looking over the glass coyly. What was she to do next? She was inexperienced in the ways of men. How strange . . . when she had spent the last four years in a house filled with women whose expertise with men was shockingly bold!

Steven sipped at the wine, then sat the glass down and began walking toward the door, feeling suddenly awkward in this young lady's presence. She seemed to have lost the ability to speak. Anyone as bashful had no business entertaining a gentleman in her room, no matter how innocent the intention.

"I will now take my leave," Steven said hoarsely from across his shoulder, not daring to take another look her way. Her loveliness—the wide sweetness of her eyes, the tempting swell of her breasts—set his loins afire, and even more so his heart. He would leave her and find some wench to release the devil itch inside him. But he would surely be thinking of Rochelle as he released his wild seed inside another. There was something haunting about her . . . a remembrance of another time, another place. He had seen such bewitching eyes and flaming hair before. But damn if he could put his finger on when.

Again panic began to rise inside Rochelle. Her inexperience was going to lose him to her. She knew it! She must stop him, one way or the other. But before she could even rise from the chair, he had slipped from the room and had closed the door between them.

"No!" she gasped, placing a hand to her cheek, aware of the flush that burned there. She knew that he had expected much more from her than she'd willingly given or offered. When she'd brought him into the room, he'd thought that before he left, he would have what men desired of women. And she now knew that if she didn't offer him this to get him back into the room, all her plans would once more go awry. She couldn't let this happen. Not even if it meant that she must let him. . . .

Afraid, yet knowing that she had no other choice, Rochelle dropped the glass to the carpet and rushed to the door and opened it. Her heart skipped a beat when she found Steven still there, outside in the corridor, as though waiting for her.

"Steven," Rochelle said in a near whisper, reaching a hand out to him.

"Are you sure?" he asked, a huskiness thick in his words, not sounding at all like him.

"Is it what you want of me?" she murmured, her face and eyes hot with excitement, though shame assailed her for her wantonness. But she must do whatever she could to make sure he didn't slip away from her.

"I never asked. . . ." he said thickly, taking her hands in his. "I only came here to see to your welfare." Then he had the urge to bite his tongue! She had offered and he was giving her the chance to back down!

"I know," she murmured, lowering her eyes. "But I am . . . willing. . . ."

"Only if you wish to," he said, again ready to kick himself for being so gallant.

Afraid to say no, afraid that he would again too quickly take his leave, Rochelle thought that she had no other choice but to agree to whatever he desired. Her knees were weak, her pulse erratic at the thought of what was to follow, but for the sake of vengeance, she, yes, was willing. She had to, somehow, get him to talk in length about his future . . . about his dreams, his desires. Perhaps afterward, when he was relaxed, he would speak at length. She would absorb each and every word. . . .

Having been without a woman for too long now, and relieved that he wouldn't have to fulfill his needs with just any street wench, Steven smiled broadly down at Rochelle when she nodded her head yes. Somehow he had read her wrong. Though she wasn't a practiced prostitute, for prostitutes knew a damn sight more about the seduction of a man, she was most surely a whore, or why would she be so willing?

Trying to hide her trembling, Rochelle avoided him as he attempted to take her hands to lead her back into the room. Her gaze fell upon the large, four-poster bed whose red velvet spread seemed to be mocking her, as though shouting out "Scarlet woman, scarlet woman!"

What would her father think if he were alive? *Anthony* would disown her for certain! How could she ever tell Anthony that she did it for the sake of her father and brother? He had thought that she had forgotten revenge long ago. How could she make Anthony understand that her nights and days had been filled with the piercing blue eyes of Steven Browning? Did she even truly understand, herself?

"You are so quiet," Steven said, closing the door behind them as Rochelle inched on into the room. He stepped before her and looked down into her eyes. "Something is wrong here. Perhaps I should leave again and this time not return."

Knowing that this was, indeed, her last chance to make him stay, Rochelle stepped closer to him and upon tiptoe, moved her lips closer to his. Her heart thundered wildly. She felt licking flames of desire rushing through her.

"You're so beautiful," Steven murmured. He drew her close against his hard frame. His lips lowered to hers in a series of sweet, teasing kisses. His fingers wove through the red silk of her hair.

Suddenly Rochelle felt very much the seductress and didn't care whether it was right or wrong. Anything this delicious had to be right. Her body was coming fully alive for the first time in her life. The mysteries of love were slowly unveiling themselves, and she couldn't deny herself. She was a woman . . . a woman with needs that had been locked inside her for twenty years. Now they were being unleashed by a perfect specimen of a man. Though he still was an enemy, and would always be as far as she was concerned, he was an enchanted enemy. . . .

Steven released her to begin undressing her. Tenderly his fingers went to the back of her dress and unfastened it. Slowly yet deliberately he lifted the loosened bodice up and away from her breasts. Rochelle stood breathless, eyes wide, her temples hammering with anxiety and fear. She had been told by Jolene that it was supposed to be painful the first time with a man, though Jolene had only heard of this, having never been with a man herself. But how could there be pain when so far, all that Rochelle felt was a sweet languor?

Steven's blue eyes seemed to intensify as he took in her bare breasts and the satin nipples stiffening beneath his gaze. As though willed to do so, his head lowered and his mouth eased over one of them. He swirled his tongue around the soft sweetness, drinking in the jasmine taste of her. He smiled to himself when he heard her quick intake of breath and then a whispered sigh as his hand molded her other breast.

"What are you doing?" Rochelle whispered, placing her hands to his head, weaving her fingers through the pale strands of his hair.

"There is more. . . ." Steven whispered against her skin.

"I really shouldn't. . . ." Rochelle found herself saying, her face flaming hot, her inner thighs now strangely paining her.

Steven raised away from her, his eyes imploring her. "I can leave now," he said thickly. "I never forced any woman. I most certainly don't want to force you."

Panic again seized her. Though she knew that what she was doing was against all that she had been taught, she was past all sense of caring. And if she bade him go, she knew she would never have the chance to be with him again. Though she didn't want to admit it, she knew that now her reasons for wanting him to stay were two. Oh, devil take her, she could not deny her body its needs! Nor could she deny her heart its need for revenge. Ah, wouldn't Steven be shocked to know her true reasons for delaying him! Perhaps he hadn't met anyone like Rochelle before . . . a woman who lived for revenge . . . and now possibly for . . . even the man she was to set vengeance upon!

"Please do not go," Rochelle whispered. She drifted toward him, unresisting, swept away on a cloud of desire. She fit her slim, sensuous body into his and kissed him with ardor. His hands sought her breasts, causing a storm of passion to build within her. She didn't rebel when he drew away from her and lowered her dress and then her petticoats. Even when he slipped her shoes off and then her stockings, she stood as if in a trance, seeing only his utter beauty, and desiring everything that he knew to give her.

In one sweep Steven had her in his arms and was carrying her to the magnificent bed. His eyes went dark with need as he looked at her body, at her perfect breasts, her slim, exquisite waist, her slender legs. Desire shot through him at the mere touch of her soft flesh. The fires of his passion burned higher within him and when the bed was reached he placed her there, as though to worship her.

Rochelle's heart raced as she watched him undress, having never seen a man undressed before. She couldn't believe that she was actually lying there, naked beneath his burning gaze. But the pulsing desire that scorched her insides again made her noncaring of anything but this man . . . and her needs.

And then he was suddenly lowering himself onto her,

her eyes having feasted long enough on his wide shoulders and broad chest. Her fingers combed the hair on his chest that was the color of wild wheat and had the texture of silk.

He then took her mouth, dazzling her senses even more with his dizzying kisses. His hands searched her body; it was already weakened with passion. He ran his fingers over her tapering calves and silken thighs, soon finding the secret heart of her passion. Rochelle moaned and opened her legs wide to his caresses; a hot fire shot through her. She eased her lips free from his and set her teeth into the flesh of his shoulder, biting down as she felt his hardness enter her. She tensed, knowing what surely must be next. She wasn't sure if she could bear the pain; he was large. But she desired him desperately; it was an instinct that came from she knew not where. All she knew was that it was a burning hunger crying to be fulfilled. . . .

"Darling, I have never desired anyone as much as I do you," Steven murmured, raining kisses along the gentle lines of her face. "Love me just a little, Rochelle. Just a little?"

Rochelle almost choked with emotion. How dare he speak the word "love" to her when she had hated him for so long? But at this moment she was confused by her feelings. Could this be love? Or was it just lust? Would she ever even know the meaning of the word "love?"

"Kiss me, Steven," she murmured, thinking this to be the best way to get past his need to hear words from her mouth that she found impossible to say. "Just hold me. Just kiss me. . . ."

Steven lowered his mouth to hers and wrapped his arms about her slim, sensuous body, lifting her up against him. The heat of his passion flamed as her lips blended against his, but when he thrust upward and found her untainted, he reared up and away from her, awestruck.

"Why, you're a . . . a virgin!" he gasped, paling. He climbed from the bed and began hurrying into his clothes. "God, Rochelle, why . . . ?"

He had never before taken a woman for the first time, though most men liked to brag of such conquests. But he didn't like to think of himself as the one to steal this sweet treat from some trusting husband! He would want the same in the woman he married.

Scrambling into his breeches, then his shoes, he looked down at Rochelle, who was now recoiling, her eyes wide and innocent. "Rochelle, I don't know what you had on your mind, but I'm not the one to do the honor," he blurted.

"Steven, please don't leave!" Rochelle cried. She jumped from the bed just as he grabbed the rest of his clothes and rushed from the room. "Oh, what am I to do?" she softly cried. "He truly thinks I'm a whore. He now surely knows that I was . . . using him. . . ."

Sobbing, she slipped hurriedly into her dress, leaving her petticoat and shoes on the floor, to rush out into the hallway, to go after Steven. Leaving the door open, she began running down the hall, almost blinded by wild tears. And when she got to the staircase and looked downward, he was there, looking up at her, beseeching her with his piercing blue eyes.

"Steven, please come back to my room with me," Rochelle said, wiping tears from her eyes. "I would die if you think badly of me."

Steven couldn't understand why Rochelle had such a driving need to please him. What was the attraction? It seemed to be a burning desire, one never known to him before.

But having his needs not yet filled and with her still so temptingly there, he moved on back up the stairs and drew her tenderly into his arms. "You are a mysterious one," he said. Their lips were drawn to one another. Rochelle whimpered, again growing languorous at his touch . . . his fiery kiss. What they had begun could not end without reaching the ultimate peak shared between man and woman. There was no need to fight it.

Steven eased away from her. His hands framed her face. "If I return to the room with you, you know that I must finish what was started," he said. "Then you will no longer be a virgin. Does not that matter to you?"

"Nothing matters now but being with you, fully with you," Rochelle said, hardly recognizing the huskiness of her voice.

"Why have you chosen me, Rochelle?" Steven asked, shaking his head, as though doubting his sanity. Was she real, or a figment of his imagination, a product of having been without a woman for so long?

"Why question something that is so good?" Rochelle whispered. "I know not how it has come about; but it has. Let us rejoice in these feelings awakened between us. Steven, I have never felt this way, ever, about any man. Only you; only you."

Tired of questioning it, desiring her ever more, he again lifted her up and into his arms and carried her back to the room. In only a matter of moments they both were undressed, their bodies tangled in a lover's embrace on the bed. Rochelle lifted her hips to meet his first thrust. She cried out with the momentary pain, then it smoothed out into a marvelous warmth that spread throughout her. She welcomed his lips as they silenced her hungry moans. She clung to his neck, letting his thrusts stir her to heights of ecstasy.

She melted into his embrace. She felt a strange thrilling sensation sending what appeared to be a million separate flames scorching her insides, and she brought her hips up closer to him, relishing the way in which he so powerfully fulfilled her.

Then a great calm washed through her, and she felt deliciously spent. But she clung to him, for he seemed to still be seeking some unknown realm of pleasure for himself. And then she felt his body stiffen and lurch and heard him emit a husky groan of pleasure, and somehow she knew that he had also reached the pinnacle of release. . . .

When he became as calm as she, he leaned up on an elbow and surprised her with a sudden question.

"I know this is a strange time to be asking, but I want to know everything about you," he murmured, giving her a brief kiss upon her sweet lips.

Rochelle stiffened with his request, finding that it somehow broke the sensuous spell she had found herself in. If she gave him the answers that he sought, she would reveal much that he did not want to hear. . . .

"You first," she said, smiling seductively up at him. "Tell me about you . . . your hopes . . . your dreams. . . ."

Six

Steven rose from the bed and slipped his breeches on, then went and picked up the wineglass from the floor where Rochelle had dropped it. He put it back on the table beside the bed, then searched inside his uniform jacket pocket until he found himself a thin cheroot cigar.

"Do you mind if I smoke?" he asked Rochelle.

She stepped lightly from the bed and drew her petticoat over her head. "No," she said, "please do as you wish." She then smiled up at him. "But only if you agree to tell me all about yourself," she quickly added. She hadn't questioned him about the scar above his left eyebrow. She hadn't dared to, fearing the mention of war. She had had enough of war to last a lifetime, though all she had actually experienced was that one day when her brother had been killed for the sake of the Confederacy.

Yes . . . she would ask him about his scar later. Much, much later. . . .

Chuckling low, Steven chomped off one end of the cigar, wet its tip, then lighted it. He went to stand over Rochelle, running his hands over her hips framed so sensuously in their satin petticoat. "What do you want to know?" he asked, smiling down at her, the cigar hanging lazily from the corner of his mouth.

Needing to distance herself from this man who could turn her insides to warm mush, Rochelle slipped away and went to the window. She looked into the distance opposite the Capitol, where muted orange streaked the sky. She knew that she should be back at her Aunt Sara's, for soon it would be dark. But she had yet to fulfill her mission. Even if it took until midnight, she would stay here with Steven to get the proper answers out of him!

Swinging around, she directed her full attention toward him. "I'm sure you don't wish to talk about the war," she murmured. "Perhaps you would like to tell me about your family?"

Steven went to the bed and sat down, positioning his back against the magnificently carved oak headboard. He stretched his long, lean legs out before him, crossing them at the ankles. Puffing on his cigar, he took on a look of dreaminess, as though his mind was wandering to another time, another place.

"Family?" he asked, removing the cigar, now looking Rochelle's way as she walked smoothly back to the bed and sat down on its edge, eagerly watching him. "You might say that I have none."

Rochelle's eyes widened. "Oh? I'm sorry," she said softly. "I didn't mean to cause you pain by having you speak of something that you'd rather not."

Steven laughed hoarsely. "No . . . it's all right," he said. "It's not what you think. It's not painful for me to talk about. You see, I ran away from home at the age of twelve, all on my own; I thought I needed adventure. My parents didn't approve and they said that my plate was the same as broken, and to not bother to come back."

"No!" Rochelle gasped, placing her hands to her cheeks. "How horrible!"

Steven shrugged. "It hasn't bothered me all that much," he said. "You see, they only wanted me there to do all the chores while my older brother sat back and read law books. I had other ideas of how I wanted to spend my life. Keeping my nose in a book or having to clean pig pens was not my idea of adventure."

"Where are you parents now?"

"Nebraska."

"Don't you ever wish to see them?" she asked, pining now for her brother and father. At times it became so painful she could hardly bear it.

"After they learned I was with the military they contacted me," he said dryly. He placed his cigar between his lips and took several angry puffs from it. "All they were interested in was being able to brag that their youngest son had become famous. They didn't contact me because they had missed me, nor to tell me that they loved me."

Rochelle moved to his side and placed a hand gently to his smooth, clean-shaven face. "Poor baby," she crooned. Then she recoiled from him, suddenly aware that he was drawing her into deeper feelings that she didn't want. How could she sympathize with him when it was *he* who had changed the course of her future by being responsible for the deaths of both her father and brother? Sometimes she wondered if she was daft! Letting him take her virginity was enough. He could have no other part of her, least of all her heart!

Steven noticed she had changed moods quickly. He reached a hand to her long, flaming tresses. Weaving his fingers through her hair, he again felt desire rising within him. Had he ever seen such a beautiful young woman? She was a seductress and it puzzled him still that she had chosen him to lose her virginity to. It was as though it had been planned . . . but that made no sense whatsoever. Why would she have any reason to pull him into a seduction?

"Tell me more," Rochelle said, looking away from his lean, bronzed, handsome face. It was enough that his hands in her hair were again threatening to set her senses spinning. How would she ever completely hate him again?

"From Nebraska I moved on to Texas, where I joined a mavericking crew," he said, dropping his hand away from her. He took the cigar from between his lips and placed it in an ashtray. "It was there that I learned to love everything about the cowboy way of life. I now plan to have my own ranch. As soon as I get things settled here in Washington, I hope to set out for Montana."

Rochelle's insides churned, her fingers began to tremble. Swallowing hard, she inched closer to him. "Montana?" she dared to say, hardly believing even now that she had pulled answers from him so easily. "Why Montana?"

"Why?" he asked, frowning. He reached and drew her up next to him. "because it is a paradise of free grass. To acquire a part of that paradise, a stockman merely places a notice in the nearest weekly newspaper, listing his brand and establishing by personal decree the extent of his range, bordering it upon creeks or familiar landmarks such as buttes or dry coulee."

" 'Coulee?' What is that?" Rochelle asked, wishing that he wouldn't run his finger along her arm so. His touch enflamed her. She didn't want to get caught up in passion again. She wanted to get the answers to her questions, then leave!

"Yes. You wouldn't know such a term as 'coulee,' would you?" Steven chuckled.

"I have never traveled any farther than Virginia, though I was born in Texas," she blurted, at once wishing she hadn't been so open. She didn't want him to know anything about her past until she was ready to tell him everything . . . but after she had had her fun with him, making his life one of complete misery.

"Oh?" he asked, sitting away from the headboard, his lovely blue eyes wide with discovery. "Was your father involved in mavericking? Or what?"

Dark shadows crossed Rochelle's face at the mere mention of her father. She wanted to shout at him that it was he who had caused her father's death! It was he who had shot and then bayoneted her brother! But she had to refrain from this. She still had a lengthy game to play with him.

"Yes. My father was a cowboy, but that was many years ago," she softly stated. "But you are forgetting my question. What is a coulee?"

"Why don't you want to talk about your past?" Steven asked, again drawing her next to him, kissing the tip of her nose.

Rochelle's insides began a slow melting. "You are right," she murmured. "I'd rather not talk about my family. Anyway, there's not much to tell."

Steven shrugged. He settled back against the headboard and leaned her into his side, holding her tightly against him. "So you want to know what a coulee is," he chuckled. "It's a small stream, a dry stream bed. It is sometimes called a gully."

Rochelle giggled. "Well, now that's simple enough," she said. She tensed when Steven leaned over and buried his lips along the delicate, vulnerable line of her neck.

"What . . . what are you doing . . . ?" she murmured, unable to stop her heart from racing.

"What do you think I'm doing?" Steven chuckled. "I'm kissing your sweet neck."

Rochelle shoved him away from her, breathing hard. "Please don't," she said, strained.

"Why not?" he asked, again reaching for her. "Why waste time?" He nodded toward the window. "Night has fallen. I could even spend the night, if you'd like."

Rochelle's insides froze. She hadn't expected him to ask that of her. Yet she'd told him that she'd paid for a full night's lodging. She scooted away from him, reaching for her dress, feeling suddenly trapped.

"Hey! Where are you going?" Steven asked, grabbing her by a wrist, yanking her back beside him.

"I . . . I suddenly remembered an appointment that I have," she mumbled, ashen.

"What sort of appointment?" he chuckled. "Darling, it's quite dark out there. No lady should be wandering the streets of Washington after nightfall. It's not safe. Remember, even the President wasn't safe, and he was guarded."

"Yes . . . the President," Rochelle murmured, an involuntary shudder coursing through her at the memory of President Lincoln lying so still in his casket.

"Remembering how quickly his life was snuffed from him makes one realize one should take advantage of every moment of life while one can," he said thickly. "Who knows from one day to the next where a body will even be? Alive and well, or in a grave?"

Rochelle shuddered visibly. "How morbid!" she gasped.

Steven moved closer and wrapped his arms about her. "I didn't mean to be," he apologized. "All I want is to make you understand that this moment we are sharing will soon be a thing of the past. Let's take advantage of what we've discovered between us. Don't you feel it? It's something almost undefinable. I need you again, Rochelle. I want you."

He gave her a hot, searing kiss. She couldn't help but writhe in response, yet she was fighting this want, this need that matched his. His fingers went to her petticoat and lowered it down and away from her breasts, then fully possessed them with his hands. His thumbs teased the peaks, causing them to stiffen and strain against his flesh.

Feeling herself newly caught up in rapture, Rochelle began shoving at his chest. She managed to get her lips free. "Please," she softly cried. "Not again. I shouldn't have . . . even . . . that first time."

Steven said nothing, just swept her into his arms and crushed her breasts against his bare chest. Rochelle's breath was stolen from her as his hand began creeping up the silent material of her petticoat, sliding up, caressing the velvety flesh, stroking the pulsing core of her womanhood. How could she have never been aware of such a sensuous part of her body before this day? It had come alive only after having been taken to a dimension of passion with Steven. And now, it had come to life again and begged to be caressed. She was becoming lost to all reason again. She only ached to be loved . . . to share with him the exquisite feelings of touches and embraces.

"You want me," Steven said huskily, now smoothing his finger over her hardened bud. "Say it, Rochelle."

She squirmed, she sighed. She let him lay her down on the bed as though she were a limp rag doll, to undress her. When she was once more nude and he was removing his breeches and standing over her beside the bed, she knew that again she would have to wait for full answers from him. Where in Montana was he going to make his residence? She had to know, or all of this would be in vain.

But no; none of this would ever be for naught. He had awakened the woman in her. He had taught her what desire was. She now knew the mystery of man and woman. But she knew that by his doing so, he had led her to possibly loving him. She didn't want this! She wanted to hate him enough to get vengeance!

No matter, though. Hate or love . . . what was the difference? She would still carry out her plans; she must. It was for her brother and father. . . .

A delicious shiver of desire raced across her flesh when Steven crept down onto the bed beside her and pulled her up and over him, so that her breasts lay upon his chest. The feel of his hard, muscled body beneath hers spurred her to run her fingers up and down the full length of his body, around to his powerful buttocks.

Steven framed her face between his hands and guided her lips downward. As he kissed her, he probed upward with his man's strength and found her open and willing to take him inside her. One gentle thrust and he was there, where he could feel a gentle warmth encircling his manhood.

With a rapid heartbeat he began his thrusts, still kissing her, smiling to himself when she emitted a soft cry of passion against his lips. The bed once more became a cradle of pleasure, a place where feelings again developed and flourished, as hands explored and mouths fed one from another. Steven relished the feel of her above him and the way she was riding him. He placed his hands to her soft hips and pressed her harder against him. They were plunging into unfathomed depths of wild, sensuous pleasure.

Rochelle was growing langorous, feeling the familiar wave of desire rising like a tempest inside her, her world melting away in his torrid embrace. The storm was building . . . building. One kiss blended into another. Her body was on fire. When he forced her lips apart and his tongue seductively entered her mouth, she was lost, helpless in surrender.

And then again it happened as it had before. Blazing, searing flashes of pleasure coated her insides, taking her to the peak of desire, then leaving her satiated and breathless. Drawing her lips away from his, she placed her cheek on his chest and waited for his own release. She felt the insides of her thighs quivering still from the pleasure that she had only moments ago felt there. She sighed. Never had any thing felt so delicious, and she knew that she was lost to feelings that she would forever want to know. . . .

Steven emitted a low groan, his body trembled violently, and then he eased her off and to his side. He touched her gently, then stretched out on his back, as though in a quiet daze.

Rochelle rose up on one elbow. She looked at his face, seeing how calm he was, ah, so handsome, with his straight, long nose, lips formed to perfection, and a gently sloping jaw. Thick blond lashes were closed over his eyes and his hair, the color of summer wheat, lay tossled about his forehead. His bronzed skin had lost the freckles that she remembered having seen the first time they had met. He now looked more mature, a man experienced of life's tragedies. Yet there was something more about him . . . a sort of triumphant look . . . a look acquired only by triumph in one's ventures. And hadn't she just become one of his conquests for a second time? She had to wonder if he always got what he went after. She knew that she tried damned hard to achieve all she desired! And still she had to pull answers out of him, though doing so would intrude upon their intimate moments.

She glanced toward the window. She saw only darkness now, and a desperation rose inside her. She knew that her Aunt Sara would be frantic. Would she have sent word to Anthony that Rochelle hadn't returned home? She had to hurry, or she would be forced to tell where she had been . . . and with whom. . . .

Lifting a forefinger to Steven's chin, she touched him lightly. "Steven, are you asleep?" she whispered, watching the stillness in which he lay. He seemed so at peace with the world . . . too calm, as far as she was concerned. She was fighting a battle with herself and she didn't like to think that he was taking lightly everything they had just shared. She couldn't help but feel used . . . yet wasn't it *she* who had used *him?*

Steven's lips moved; he sighed. "Do you know how many nights I spent on the ground these past four years? Ah, a bed . . . it feels like a cloud. Don't awaken me, Rochelle. Just let me drift."

She frowned. "Steven . . . you never did tell me where you were going to settle in Montana," she murmured, tracing his jawline with her forefinger. She tensed, waiting for his answer. Again she thought him to be asleep. He was breathing so smoothly, his eyelids weren't even fluttering.

"Giltedge," he said, yawning sleepily.

Rochelle's eyes widened; she rose to a sitting position, hardly able to believe that he had actually given her a name. Then she frowned. She knew no town named Giltedge! Where on earth could it be?

"That's a lovely name for a western town," she further tormented. "Where . . . where is it located, Steven?"

He didn't seem to notice that she was prodding him for further answers. He was too busy yawning, trying to get comfortable on his side, his back to her. But then he answered her. "Giltedge?" he whispered, already half asleep. "It's close to Fort Benton. . . ."

His words drifted off to be replaced a soft snoring. Rochelle clasped her hands together, her heart soaring, her lips set into a wide grin. She had finally found out all she needed to know. She could return victorious to her Aunt Sara's, then somehow get Anthony interested in the town of Giltedge. She could say that she liked the sound of the name. It was intriguing . . . as if the town's boundaries might be outlined with gold. There were many people rushing to Montana digging for gold. Perhaps that was how this town got its name?

But she would come up with the right way to entice Anthony later. Now she must find a way to leave the room without Steven knowing. When he awakened, he would find her gone, and then she would be a thing of mystery to him until their paths crossed again in Montana . . . in Giltedge, Montana. . . .

Hugging her knees to her chest, Rochelle anxiously watched him for any sign of wakefulness. But he was breathing too peacefully, even snoring, to be even partially awake.

"Now is the time to leave," she whispered to herself. "He's oblivious now of anything but dreams."

With a pounding heart and trembling fingers, Rochelle hurriedly dressed. She slipped on her hood and put the veil into her purse. After taking one last lingering look at Steven, and feeling a rush of desire flow through her at his handsome nakedness, she forced herself to rush away. She hurried out onto Pennsylvania Avenue, where she boarded a carriage that would take her far away from the man that had stolen more than she dared let herself admit.

But at least her plan had taken root; even more than that, it seemed to have planted a seed in her heart, a seed that would perhaps grow, fully blossom into love, if she would allow it. . . .

Rochelle glided up the great front steps of her aunt's house, breathless. In the windows warm lights reflected gold out onto the lawn, yet there weren't the usual guests this night. Most of Sara's clients were now men who had idolized President Lincoln, and out of respect of him, most had stayed away from their night of frolicking. Rochelle was glad. She could make an entrance without too much notice being drawn her way. She wasn't usually away until after dark.

Yet she had to know that she would surely be pounced upon the minute she opened the door. Probably Anthony was there, pacing the floor, worrying about her. She had had time to come up with a clever story as to where she had been and why she had been detained. She only hoped that no one could tell that she had been with a man . . . and had gone to paradise and back with him. As astute as her Aunt Sara was about men, Rochelle had true reason to be concerned!

Tiptoeing, she walked on toward the oak door and slowly opened it. Barely breathing, she stepped on inside, then blinked her eyes wildly when she found both her aunt and Anthony standing there, their arms folded angrily across their chests.

"Where have you been, young lady?" Anthony growled, his dark face distorted by a frown. "Do you know the danger of being out after dark? This is the first time you've done this. Where have you been?"

Anger rose in hot flashes inside Rochelle. Here she was twenty and they still treated her as a stupid child! She should shout to them that she was now a woman in every sense of the word . . . that she didn't need their coddling, their protection!

But knowing that they only did this out of love for her, she sighed and slipped her hood from her head, and then the cape from her shoulders. "I'm sorry if I've worried you," she said, placing the cape over the back of a chair, and her purse on a table. "The time got away from me. I looked up and suddenly it was dark."

"Rochelle, where were you, honey?" Sara asked, going to her, placing a hand beneath her chin, to force Rochelle to look directly into her eyes.

Rochelle's stomach lurched; she did not feel safe beneath her aunt's close scrutiny. She squirmed away, her back to Sara, fidgeting with a tassel which hung about a drawn-back drape. Then she gave Anthony a half-glance. "I went to the library in Washington," she murmured. "I was reading the recent newspapers from Montana . . . all the latest news. Since we are talking so much of traveling to Montana, shouldn't I know all there is to know about it?"

Anthony kneaded his chin contemplatingly. "Hmm," he uttered. "Not a bad idea, Rochelle. I should have thought of it myself. What'd you find out?"

Rochelle sighed with relief, then turned and fully faced Anthony. "I found out the name of a town that sounded fascinating," she blurted, going to Anthony to grab onto his arm. *"Giltedge!* Anthony, doesn't it sound wonderful? I bet the whole town in surrounded by gold! Don't you think the name is intriguing? And it's not far from Fort Benton. I know. I read all about it. Do you think we might consider making it our destination?"

"It's possible," Anthony chuckled, glad for her enthusiasm. He had began to hunger more and more to leave this part of the country behind him and move out west, where he could again become useful. There had been too many years already wasted. He truly felt alive only when out on the range, working with cattle. If it hadn't been for Daniel and his family needing his companionship, he would have returned long ago. And now that Rochelle was older and capable of fending for herself, he saw no reason whatsoever to delay.

"So? When do we leave?" Rochelle said, her eyes drinking in the excitement now lighting Anthony's face.

Anthony laughed wholeheartedly. "Hey! Not so fast," he said. "We've plans to make, you know. And I've sent Jake ahead, to scout the land for us. He may find land better suited for us than Giltedge; if so, he will more than likely advise me to settle there."

The smile faded from Rochelle's face. "But Anthony, I truly would like to settle close to Giltedge," she persisted.

Anthony looked up. "Is there more to this than you're tellin' me?" he questioned, taking her hand in his. "Why this sudden persistence to settle in a town that you only just read about? Why should it make any difference one way or the other?"

Rochelle slipped her hands from his and walked quietly away from him; she had appeared too eager. "I guess it doesn't," she shrugged. Then she turned and boldly faced him. "But I do wish you would consider it over any other town. I loved what I read about it, Anthony. It has many establishments, whereas so many towns in Montana don't. We want to be able to have someplace close by where we can purchase supplies regularly."

"Yes, you're right," Anthony agreed. "Seems you've done your homework all right."

"Then what are you going to do about Jake? What if he comes back with different ideas than what we want?" she tested.

Anthony placed his hands on Rochelle's shoulders. "Honey, I haven't told you yet . . . but I plan to go on out to Montana myself, to meet Jake at Fort Benton," he said. "I can decide then what is best for us."

"You are going on ahead without me?" she gasped. "Anthony, you wouldn't. . . ."

"You will follow shortly after," he said. He walked away from her and gave Sara a half-glance. "And hopefully even Sara?"

Sara shook her head. "Anthony, you know better than that," she said dryly. "We've already discussed that."

Anthony shrugged. "But, yes, Rochelle, I'm leaving . . . soon. I'd like to at least get a house ready for your arrival."

Rochelle shook her head, unhappy with this new turn of events. "I wanted to be a part of it right from the first," she said disdainfully.

"You'd want to help build a ranch house?" Anthony chuckled.

"I could stay in a hotel until the house is completed," she argued.

"Rochelle, I know that you're used to getting your way," Anthony said impatiently. "But this one time, you will just have to practice patience."

Rochelle sighed disconsolately, yet she knew that she had won enough to make the waiting pleasurable. . . .

Seven

The moon whitewashed the roses in the garden; the fragrance was as powerful as any perfume, it seemed, set free from a bottle. Anthony walked beside Sara, his arm possessively about her waist. He knew that this was his last chance to try to convince her to travel to Montana along with him and Rochelle. He knew that once he and Rochelle left Alexandria, they would never return; it didn't seem right to think that Sara would never been seen again, no longer a part of his life, when she was now something that he had begun to depend on.

He hadn't wanted to become entangled in feelings for a woman of questionable repute, yet it had been too hard to deny himself what Sara so openly offered him, once even confessing to him that he was the only one who now benefited from her special skills.

She had said that since he had entered her life, she needed no other man. Yet she had never spoken the word "love" to him. Anthony had wondered about her past: what could have hardened her enough to make her reluctant to give fully of herself to a man?

Anthony sighed. He was torn. He wanted Sara as his wife, if he could only convince her to leave her questionable life behind her. He did love her, and one experienced this sort of love but once in a lifetime. Perhaps he might be loving the wrong lady. . . .

"It's peaceful tonight, isn't it, Anthony?" Sara said, looking up at him. He seemed to be in deep thought; she could only guess about what. She knew to expect him to ask her again tonight to change her way of living, to travel with him to Montana. How could she convince him that she would never be happy anywhere but Alexandria? She loved her independence. If she were to live with Anthony as his wife, she would feel stifled, imprisoned.

"I'm sure the whole world feels the strange stillness," Anthony said thickly. "With the assassination of the President, one wonders who is or is not safe in the world."

He looked down at her, trying not to be swept up in her earthy loveliness. "Peaceful?" he questioned. "Yes, the stillness we feel tonight seems peaceful. But I don't look to it as anything but a quiet fear."

"You talk as though you approved of President Lincoln," Sara said, remembering how life was to change for everyone because of Lincoln and what he had managed to succeed at doing before his death. If not for him, surely there would have been no Civil War. If not for him, surely much of the country would now be intact, instead of in rubble.

But she didn't want to dwell on ugliness. Here at the estate, everything was still beautiful, undisturbed by the ravages of war.

"I guess you know I have other things on my mind than talk of Lincoln," Anthony said hoarsely.

Sara's mouth hardened into a straight line. She tilted her nose, looking away from him. "Yes," she murmured, "I know."

"And you refuse even to discuss it," Anthony growled. "Is that what your sudden coldness is all about?"

"You might say that," Sara said, easing out of his grasp. She went to the gazebo set far back from her house and sat down on a plush cushioned seat, stiffening when he just as quickly sat down beside her.

But when his hand went to her throat, his fingers touching her gently there, moving downward to caress her generously exposed bosom, her breath was stolen from her and she saw that he knew how to melt her resistance. In him, she knew excitement. She always experienced flames of desire when he touched her. She even wondered how she was ever going to be able to live without him. . . .

"Then, my dear, let me warm you in the only way I know how," Anthony said huskily, his lips scalding her flesh where his fingers had just been. He looked up at her hazel eyes. And he was glad to see that she was already unfastening her dress from behind. The gazebo had become a secret sort of hideaway for them, a place to share moments away from the house that was an unfortunate reminder of just how many men she had shared it with.

"Yes," Sara said, her voice thick with feeling. She let the dress drop from her shoulders, baring her breasts to his searching lips. A shudder coursed through her, and her pulse began to race. "Anthony, please wait for me to undress completely. Darling, I want all of you . . . Tomorrow. . . ."

"Yes," he said flatly. "Tomorrow I leave for Montana. You do know what that means, don't you?"

"I can't bear to think about it," Sara murmured. "Please, let's just pretend there is no tomorrow . . . that there's only tonight."

"Your problem is that you don't live for the morrow,"

he argued. "You've learned to live just for *now.* It's not realistic, Sara. *Now* sometimes can be no more than a figment of one's imagination."

"Oh?" she said, her eyes wide. "I am that? Only a figment of your imagination?"

"What I meant is that you only *imagine* that now is what is important to you, so you pretend that it is all that you have," Anthony said, placing his hands to the silken curves of her thighs as she stood and let her dress drop to her ankles. "I'm afraid that one day you will be in for a rude awakening. Things won't continue to be so easy for you. In your profession, much can happen quickly."

"What do you mean?" she softly challenged.

"I've known of women like you . . . uh . . . who run such houses . . . to get run out of town."

Sara's eyes widened and then she threw her head back into a rowdy laugh. Then she sobered, and placed her hands to Anthony's cheeks. "My darling, now who has an overactive imagination?" she purred. "Surely you know such a thing can never happen to me."

Anthony rose to stand before her, his hands taking in the roundness of her breasts, their utter softness causing his loins to become enflamed. He bent over and pressed his lips softly against hers and drew her into him, her mound of fur crushed against his risen male strength, though his layer of clothes between them was like a wall, stopping any further love play.

Sara reached her fingers to his hair and wove them through its dark thickness. She whispered between kisses, "Don't you think we'd have more fun if you removed your damn clothes?"

"I thought you'd never ask," he chuckled.

Stepping back away from her, he shed each piece of clothing one at a time, all the while absorbing her silken pinkness as the moonlight played softly over her body. Her auburn hair was circled in neat rows of waves atop her head, and a few ringlets cascaded about her round face, framing her always dangerous-looking hazel eyes, her slightly Roman nose, and her pretty mouth.

When completely nude, Anthony took a step toward Sara and lifted his hands to her hair, removing the pins from it, loosening it until it all hung long and beautiful down her back.

And then he couldn't bear it any longer. He had to have her breasts crushed against his bare flesh. He wanted to feel her tonight, to feel her completely, to memorize the feeling and carry it with him in the coming lonely weeks and months.

"Come to me, baby," he said huskily. He jerked her body onto his, groaning when he felt the taut tips of her nipples relax against his chest, feeling the soft auburn curls between her thighs work up against the hardness of his leg.

Sara's hands began moving seductively over him, relishing the touch of his muscled back, down lower to the smoothness of his powerful buttocks. Her lips reached up and found his mouth open and ready. She eased her tongue inside and played with his; his hands went to her soft hips and lifted her up and onto his risen man's strength. Quite experienced in this way to make love, she placed her legs about him and sighed shakily with pleasure as he began to plunge himself deeply inside her.

Clinging now about his neck, Sara cried out her joy. "Darling, make it last forever. Darling. . . ."

His mouth scorched her, silencing her words. He worked inside her with quick, sure movements, all the while his fingers digging into her flesh, holding her solidly in place against him. She writhed in response. Soft moans repeatedly surfaced from between her lips.

And then he suddenly released himself from inside her and placed her on the floor. Like a puppet she let him stretch her out on cushions on the floor and again enjoyed his love play as his lips began a slow worship of her body. Desire swelled inside her as she let her eyes take in his wide shoulders tapering to narrow hips and then the powerful part of him that set her senses to reeling. She reached a hand to his manhood and encircled it and skillfully began moving on him, all the while his lips were setting her flesh afire and his hands were caressing her breasts.

Turning so that he would be more accessible to her, Anthony let out a soft groan when he felt the wet tip of her tongue snake across his throbbing hardness. And when her lips fully possessed him, he quit breathing momentarily, absorbing the full pleasure of the moment, then emitted a long, quivering sigh.

He then reciprocated and let his mouth find the soft honey dew of her womanhood. Together they made passion peak, and when Anthony could bear no more, he again repositioned his body and lunged himself back inside her.

He kissed her torridly, her hot and hungry mouth trembling against his lips, her hips rising to meet his eager thrusts. His hands reached beneath her and lifted her even higher. She locked her legs about his back and pressed her love mound hard against him, the power of their need building. Theirs was not a gentle loving. It was that of wildness . . . an unleashed fury which always overwhelmed them both.

In a blaze of urgency they both reached the ultimate height of pleasure together, she still anchored fiercely against him, while their bodies quaked and shook and then became gradually calm. . . .

Panting, Anthony still lay above her, not wanting to give up the lover's lock in which they lay. He could never get enough of her generous breasts or of what she offered him where she was so warm. His lips even now moved as if on command to kiss her breast. While his one hand caressed it, his lips covered over the taut tip, drawing a renewed moan of intense pleasure from deeply inside Sara.

His free hand traveled lower to where her love mound was pressed against him. Working his fingers between their bodies he began a slow, teasing caress. He watched as her eyes closed with rapture. Her tongue was slowly licking her lips and she threw her head back as another spasm of release flooded through her.

Feeling the contractions against his stilled manhood caused a renewed flame of passion to be lighted there. He wove his fingers through her hair and guided her lips to his, and while ardently kissing her he again began his eager thrusts, seeking another cloud of desire to float upon in only a matter of minutes.

Sara could feel his animal heat. She coiled her arms about his neck and began lifting her hips, again surrendering herself to an intense sexual excitement. She knew that she could go on all night. She was insatiable, as was he. . . .

And after they had again reached that plateau and were fully dressed, Anthony guided Sara back out beneath the soft splash of the moonlight.

Smiling, he reached and let his fingers caress the long waves of her hair. "Seems you've misplaced your hairpins," he said. "Now won't someone be surprised when they find them scattered all over the floor of the gazebo?"

"That wouldn't be the first time," Sara laughed, leaning into his embrace, soaking him up, all of him. Tomorrow, she would lose him forever.

Strolling down a path which led them to the banks of the Potomac River, Anthony was trying to get the courage to again ask Sara to be his wife. How could she deny them a future of what they had found together? Surely she couldn't let it slip away so easily. Yet each time he had asked, she had given him an adamant "no." How could he get her to change her mind?

"Sara," he suddenly said, swinging around to face her. "I have to ask you again. Sell this place. Go to Montana with me and Rochelle. Let me make an honest woman of you."

Sara's eyes widened. Her mouth dropped open. "An honest woman?" she gasped, her face reddening in anger. "Anthony, of all the things you could have said at this moment, that was the worst!"

She stomped away from him and went to stand at the river's edge, hugging herself, fending off the chill wind that blew across the water. She was trembling. She hated it when Anthony made her feel like a cheap tramp. Honest woman, indeed!

Anthony went to her and drew her around to look intensely down onto her lovely face. "Sara, don't be so sensitive," he growled. "You know what I was leading up to. Why get your dander up just because I used the wrong approach?"

"Any approach would be wrong," she sighed. "Anthony, don't waste your breath trying to convince me of something that I refuse to do."

"Then you are forcing me to do something that is going to make Rochelle quite uncomfortable," he growled, releasing her from his arms to glower.

Sara stepped closer to him and looked up at him.

"What about Rochelle?" she murmured. "What are you talking about?"

Anthony took her by the shoulders. "It will be in Montana as it was here," he grumbled. "It would not look respectable for me and Rochelle to live under the same roof unless we are man and wife."

Sara paled; her insides grew cold. "You aren't saying that you are . . . going to encourage Rochelle to marry you?"

Anthony raked his fingers nervously through his hair. "No, nothing like that," he said.

"Then what, Anthony?"

"We will have to pretend to be man and wife," he said in a rush of words.

"Lord!" Sara asked.

"It's the only way," Anthony said, kicking at a rock with the toe of his boot. He then again looked at her. "Unless, of course, you agree to go to Montana with us and be my wife. Everything would work out fine if you would do that. Is it such a terrible thing . . . to think on being my wife?"

"Lord, Anthony," Sara said, taking a wide step away from him, again to stare across the dark body of water. "I do not have the same need to please Rochelle that you do. Why should I leave my way of life just because of her?"

She turned and boldly faced him. "That's the way it truly is, don't you know?" she said hoarsely. "Everything you do is prompted by the fact that you are doing it for Rochelle. You would always place her best interests before mine. You have some need to . . . to overprotect her. And what you feel for me is . . . just lust. How could that be a basis for a good marriage?"

Anthony took her hands in his and squeezed them. "Everything about our relationship, Sara, is good," he said hoarsely. "Lust? You know there is more than that. It's more than just a mere attraction. I love you. And as for Rochelle, I owe it to Daniel to see that she is looked after properly, at least until she finds a young man who can take over where I leave off."

He drew her into his arms and hugged her tightly. His lips sought and found hers, kissing her passionately. He could feel her defenses crumbling and somehow this gave him just a fraction of hope. Perhaps once he and Rochelle got to Montana, Sara would miss him so much that she would have to follow. For a while he would postpone this make-believe marriage to Rochelle, yet they would have to say they were betrothed and were waiting for a certain minister's arrival to do the honors.

With passion searing his loins, Anthony let desire take over, leaving his worries of Rochelle . . . Montana . . . even of Sara's rejection of him behind. He lowered Sara to the ground and again they found heaven in one another's arms. Tomorrow would take care of itself. . . .

Eight

Aboard the riverboat *Lady*, moving up the Missouri River, Rochelle stood on the top deck at the rail, strangely at peace with herself. The river had reached out and hypnotized her, making her momentarily forget why she was going to Montana . . . to purposely seek out Steven Browning.

Sometimes in the morning fog, the river, the shore, the sky, and everything else would be one soft gray mass, broken only occasionally by a charcoal gray line that would turn out to be the shoreline, a tree, or a drifting log. The spray from the river washed against Rochelle's face. She could smell and feel the water. The warm air was soft.

After the long train ride from Washington to St. Louis, the journey by riverboat was eagerly welcomed. Though a slow way to travel, going by steamboat was not only the most comfortable, but also the safest way to travel on to Montana.

The river was an undulating, never-ending stream that seemed to stretch on forever in front of and behind Rochelle in a vast, pearl-gray mist. Yes, Rochelle was filled with contentment, a tiny speck in an ordered vastness. The only thing that was missing was the presence of Anthony. He had gone on ahead as he'd said he would and now waited for her to play the betrothed once she arrived in Giltedge. But for how long could they pretend without raising eyebrows? How long would it take Sara to get wise and realize just how much of a man she was saying no to? How could anyone refuse Anthony anything? He was one fine catch . . . one fine gentleman like no other, as far as Rochelle was concerned.

Yet there had also been Steven Browning. Though he had willingly seduced her, he had proven to be a gentleman in his own right, even though he was a damn Yankee!

Rochelle shook her head to clear her thoughts. "What am I doing?" she whispered to herself. "I vowed not to let my thoughts wander to that man and the magic I found in his arms. I must hate him, nothing else. I've so much to do; my task is to make his life miserable."

But now she wasn't even sure that he had settled on a ranch near Giltedge, as he had spoken openly of doing. Plans changed; in this day and age, it was hard to plan an orderly future without something going awry. So she knew to expect chaos even of her own future. That would be more realistic than to think the best to happen, and then be disappointed.

"But I must keep hoping," she said, wiping a spray of water from her face.

It was shortly after dawn. The sun made a huge rainbow in the deep, misty fog. Out of the rainbow a squadron of jacksnipe suddenly banked and veered in perfect formation, their white wing patches flashing.

When the sun finally burned the mist away, revealing a bright blue sky, Rochelle stretched her arms above her head and yawned. She'd awakened long before dawn to take a private stroll on this "floating wedding cake," as she'd branded the riverboat, with its many fancy decks. There were many places for watching the river and plenty of time in which to do it.

In her simple cotton dress, worn more for comfort than for appearance, and with her hair long and free down her back, Rochelle began walking down the full length of the deck, sighing. She raised her eyes to the sky, never having felt so free. As the breeze whipped around her, the long skirt of her dress wrapped and then fell around her ankles. She could feel the building heat of the sun on her chest where her dress dipped low at the bosom. She hugged herself, she tossed her hair and wisps of red tangled around and blew into the corners of her eyes.

Now that the sun was bright and rising higher in the sky, she could smell the grass baking along the shore and hear the cheerful sound of grasshoppers singing. The brown river was oddly silent, curving and twisting in its southeasterly course between banks of blackberry brambles and feathery goldenrod. Great trees hugged the channel. The Missouri River had been born in the western mountains and had cut a powerful path through stone, carving deep clefts in rock walls on both banks.

Rochelle had enjoyed this time alone but now began noticing others drifting up on the upper deck from their cabins. Feeling an emptiness in her stomach, she decided to go back to her cabin, where she usually ate her morning meal with Jolene and Jolene's mother, Priscilla.

So that Rochelle would not have to travel alone, Sara had sacrificed her own personal maid and her maid's daughter to the trip. At least by doing this she had showed concern for Rochelle's welfare.

"She does care for me," Rochelle whispered, smiling

to herself. "Now I know it. She wouldn't have sent Priscilla along if she didn't; Jolene, perhaps . . . but not Priscilla."

Priscilla had been Sara's private maid ever since Sara was a child living with her brother and family. Sara had gone into business for herself and her mother and father had died tragically not long after, and Priscilla had become not only Sara's maid again, but also a substitute mother.

"Yes, it is a sacrifice on Sara's part, and I will forever be in her debt," Rochelle thought.

But she knew not how she could repay such a debt if Sara so stubbornly refused to travel to Montana. . . .

Suddenly Rochelle's eyes became riveted: there was something familiar about a man who was now leaning his full weight against the rail only a few steps from her. With his back to her, she could see his blond hair feathered by the breeze, lifted from his collar. His neck was bare, muscular, and browned by exposure.

He was broad-shouldered and thin-flanked, standing six-feet in his cowboy boots. His buckskin breeches were fringed at the seams and gathered at the waist with a wide leather belt, and he wore a plaid shirt which strained at the shoulders.

Without even seeing him from the front, Rochelle knew that this man's eyes were piercing blue and that his jaw was gently rounded . . . she even knew that his face displayed high cheekbones and a proud, long nose. For she had no doubt whatsoever that this man was, indeed, Steven Browning!

A slow panic began to rise within her. What was Steven Browning doing on this riverboat? She would have expected him to have gone by way of another route. And what was she to do? The journey would be long. There would be no way to keep him from finding out that she was also a passenger. And it wasn't in her plans for him to know. How could she explain why she was going there? She had wanted to spring the surprise on him at the right moment—which most certainly was not now!

She felt glued to the spot. She was afraid that he might catch any movement out of the corner of his eye, and that he would then be drawn around to look her way. But the longer she stood there, the more threatened she became—not only by the thought of discovery, but by her feelings for him. She was remembering their last moments together. Oh, how he had a way of sending her to heaven! A mere touch and she would be gone again. What was she to do? How could she avoid him?

"Rochelle!"

Her stomach lurched when Jolene's shrill voice spoke suddenly from behind her. Rochelle's fingers circled into tight fists, knowing that everyone on the deck surely had heard, for Jolene's voice carried far.

Turning with a jerk, Rochelle glared at Jolene with a set jaw. She placed a forefinger to her lips. "Shh!" she said. "Jolene, please. . . ."

But she knew that it was too late. She could feel Steven's eyes on her without even turning to look his way. He had heard and now he saw. And all she could do was pretend that she didn't know that he had even been there.

With her heart pounding and her throat suddenly dry, she took Jolene by the arm and began guiding her down the flight of stairs.

"Land's sakes, Rochelle," Jolene fussed. "What are you doin'? You're actin' mighty peculiar." She tried to pull her arm free, wincing. "Rochelle, you're hurtin' my arm. What's the matter? Did I do somethin' wrong?"

"You could say that," Rochelle grumbled, sidling closer to Jolene. "But I can't explain things right now. Just you keep walking. I've got to get to my cabin as quickly and quietly as possible."

"Did some man cause you trouble, Rochelle?" Jolene whispered, looking over her shoulder. "Did a man make improper advances? Is that why you're seein' the need to return to your cabin in such a hurried fashion?"

"Like I said," Rochelle whispered harshly, "I don't want to talk about it now. So just keep walking. I've got to get to my cabin, fast."

She was afraid to look behind her, afraid that Steven was following her. Several months had passed since their last encounter. Even if he had recognized her, would he even care that she was there? She had slipped away from him that night without even a goodbye.

But she knew that he had wanted to see her again. No two people shared so intensely what they had shared without caring, at least a little. She knew that she had found herself caught up in feelings for him. She had even let the word "love" enter her thoughts these past months. Somehow the word "love" seemed to fashion the same sort of emotions inside one's heart as did hate. She had to learn how to separate the two feelings when with Steven Browning. Both were strong inside her. Which would win in the end? She only knew which *should* win. For the sake of her father and brother, there was only one way to feel about Steven Browning!

When she reached the lower deck and finally felt safe inside the cabin, Rochelle leaned heavily against the closed door, breathing hard. Perspiration beaded her brow; her palms were clammy. But it was the erratic beat of her heart that disturbed her the most. She knew that it was because she had seen the man of her dreams again . . . and she couldn't deny the rush of desire that had overwhelmed her when realizing who he was.

"Now you can tell me," Jolene said, clasping her dark, slim hands before her as she anxiously peered at Rochelle's flushed face. "Mercy, Rochelle, you should see your face. It's the color of the sun, it's so red. And your eyes! My, but they are troubled!"

Rochelle had finally caught her breath. She wiped her brow with the back of her hand, then smiled down at Jolene. She knew that she had shared most everything these past years with her maid and companion. But Jolene had yet to know the intimate details about the man whose photograph lay on the table beside Rochelle's bed now that neither Anthony nor Sara were there to question her about it.

Jolene's tiny face was framed by black curls, and her black dress with its white collar made her look even smaller than she was. Her shoulders slumped, giving in to the rheumatism which plagued her. Yet she was still as beautiful as before and was ever so sweet.

"I think my plans have just gone awry," Rochelle suddenly blurted. She glided on across the room and picked up Steven's military photograph, looking down at it. "Damn, why did he have to travel by riverboat? What am I to do? I know that he saw me. What am I to say to him?"

Jolene placed a hand to the small of her back as she went to stand beside Rochelle to look down at the photograph. "Who you speakin' 'bout, Rochelle?" she asked, her eyes wide. "Does it have anythin' to do with that picture you've had all this time?"

Rochelle ran a finger over the photograph, feeling a sensual warmth rising between her thighs. The photograph had never been a good substitute, but it had been there when she needed to remember the delicious feelings that she'd shared with this man, her enemy. Enchanted enemy. Yes, that adequately described him.

"Yes . . . it has everything to do with this man," she said softly. "Jolene, he's on board this riverboat. I didn't expect to see him again until Montana."

"Montana?" Jolene gasped. "Was he supposed to be there? Did Massa Anthony know he was going to be there? Rochelle, I don't understand. Who is this man? What is he to you?"

Rochelle saw that it was time to confide in someone, and Jolene was the best candidate for such confessions. There would be no getting around it any longer. It was best to explain to Jolene now, for it would have to be done sooner or later. Steven would seek her out for questioning once he was sure that it was she. And she could expect many questions from him!

Rochelle first asked for Jolene's cooperation in keeping this between the two of them. Even Jolene's mother wasn't to be told, though it might become almost impossible to keep the truth from her if Steven got persistent in his pursuit.

And after Jolene had given the word, Rochelle told all. . . .

"This is the man who shot your brother?" Jolene said in a surprised whisper, her eyes wide.

"And also the man responsible for my father's sudden heart attack," Rochelle said venomously.

"And you plan to pretend to be a friend to this man?" Jolene said, not understanding what Rochelle had planned.

"I only wished to do so after arriving in Montana," Rochelle sighed, once again peering down at the photograph. "Now what am I to do? I can't stay hidden away in this cabin for the rest of the journey. I couldn't bear it, Jolene. I so love to mingle with the passengers. There's even to be a dance tonight in the Grand Saloon, with an orchestra."

Jolene set her lips firmly. "You'll be foolish to let that man ruin your riverboat excitement," she fussed. "Let him see you. Begin our little game now, on the boat." She took on an impish look as she giggled. "It could even be fun, don't you think? Dance with him. Flirt with him. Then, when you get to Montana, the scene would already be set for your further games of annoyance with him."

"But how can I explain why I am here? When I tell him I am on my way to Montana, surely he will get suspicious. He will remember that he told me that he was going to make *his* residence there."

"Now why would that man believe you planned any of this?" Jolene said, her eyes flashing with excitement, enjoying sharing Rochelle's devious plan. "Why, Rochelle, you're only a helpless lady, going to the man who paid your way to Montana so you can become his wife. It's done all the time. Wives are acquired by mail order. Can't you see? You can say that you are a mail-order bride. It is already planned for you and Anthony to pretend to be betrothed to one another, to make it look respectable for you to live under the same roof."

Rochelle's heart began to pound wildly. She placed the photograph on the table, then spun around and grabbed Jolene's hands and squeezed them. "Jolene, you're an absolute angel!" she cried. "What you just said, I know it will work. It's perfect. Why didn't I think of it?"

"Then you will plan to go to the dance and even let this man know you're on board?" Jolene said anxiously, her heart racing with excitement. What fun this could be . . . this toying with a man's affections. Now if only Jolene's mama could be kept from finding out! Her mama had accompanied Rochelle and Jolene on this trip to protect them from rogues such as Steven Browning. But it would be up to Jolene to convince her mother that Steven Browning was a respectable man, one to trust.

"Yes!" Rochelle giggled. "I will. Oh, what a surprise Steven will get when I tell him about my betrothed waiting for me in Montana!"

Then her smile faded. Perhaps telling him about her "betrothed" could spoil everything. What if the gentlemanly side of him made him step away from her, to leave her alone? But she had no other choice than to chance it.

Then she again remembered the last time they had been together, and how she had sneaked from the room. How was she to explain that?

It would be the respectable side of her that she would say had made her leave him . . . she had suddenly been plagued by guilt for having let him take her innocence. Yes, that was perfect; that would be something that he could believe. He had seen that she had been almost timid with him. He had surely wondered about why she had allowed him to seduce her . . . as he would continue to wonder now about why she did anything.

She smiled to herself. She liked being a woman of mystery. That made her vengeance even more sweet. . . .

A light tap on the door made Rochelle's knees become suddenly weak. She looked wild-eyed toward Jolene, whose eyes were riveted on the door.

"It's him!" Rochelle whispered, placing her hands to her cheeks, feeling how hot they were. She was torn . . . a part of her wanted to see him, another wanted to shut him entirely from her life. Her feelings for him forever confused her! All she wanted was vengeance . . . nothing more. Yet her heart seemed to betray her wants . . . her needs. . . .

"Rochelle? Jolene? Are you girls in there?" Priscilla asked in her gravelly voice. "You open this door immediately, do you hear?"

Rochelle took a step backward, swallowing hard. It wasn't Steven at all; it was Priscilla! She sounded mad enough to kill, and Rochelle understood why: in her haste to get away from Steven, she had quickly latched the cabin door's lock! Priscilla didn't like being locked out, even though it was Rochelle's place to do as she pleased, since Priscilla was only her maid.

But she respected Priscilla as she did Jolene. Rushing to the door, she threw the latch back and swung the door open wide. Her face was flushed, her eyes were full of apology. "Priscilla, I didn't mean to lock you out," she quickly explained. "I just locked that door by accident."

Priscilla stomped on into the room, showing her authority . . . authority given her by Sara Jackson! It was her place to protect Rochelle, and protect her she would! She closed the door behind her.

Her face dark, leathery, and lined with age, Priscilla looked suspiciously from Jolene to Rochelle. She placed her hands on her hips. "What you two up to?" she spat. "Is it a man?"

Rochelle gave Jolene a quick glance, then smiled sheepishly at Priscilla. "A man?" she said weakly. "Why, Priscilla, why on earth would you ask such a question? Man, indeed!"

"Cause a man is goin' from cabin to cabin' askin' for you, Rochelle," Priscilla hissed. "He come to my

cabin askin' for you. Who is this man? Why is he askin' for you?"

"No! He isn't!" Rochelle whispered, paling. She now remembered that she hadn't bought passage on the *Lady* under her own name. Anthony had advised her to take it under his, to protect her from men who might check the passenger list hunting for a woman to take advantage of. It was best to use a man's name on the passenger list, and she had.

Yes, that had to be why Steven was going from cabin to cabin. He had definitely recognized her and was now determined to find her, even if it meant pestering everyone on board.

"What'd you say beneath your breath?" Priscilla said, suspicious.

Rochelle laughed nervously. "Oh, nothing," she said. "I'm just wondering why any man would be asking for me. How would he . . . even . . . know my name?"

She knew she wouldn't be able to keep Priscilla in the dark for long. Would Priscilla approve of what Rochelle was planning to do, once she knew? Would she vow to keep her silence, as Jolene had? Rochelle wasn't yet sure of Priscilla's loyalty. She had only recently become her traveling companion and maid. . . .

A loud knock on the door drew Rochelle's breath from her. Suddenly she felt trapped between two forces. Priscilla and . . . and surely it was Steven at the door! She covered her mouth with her hands, not knowing what to do. She looked wildly from Jolene to Priscilla. Then she moved quickly, to hide behind where the door would swing open.

"Go to the door. Don't tell anyone I'm here," she whispered to them.

"You cain't hide forever," Priscilla scolded. "What has this man done to scare you, Rochelle? Has he made improper advances? If so, I shall inform the captain. . . ."

Rochelle frantically shook her head back and forth. "No!" she whispered harshly. "Don't do anything yet, Priscilla, except tell that man . . . if it is that man . . . that I'm not here. I'll tell you everything as soon as he leaves . . . I promise."

Shaking her head, Priscilla lumbered over to the door when the knocking began again, this time even more determinedly. She eased the door open a crack and peered out, frowning. "Young man, what do you want?" she scolded. "You disturbed me once this mornin'. I'm busy now with my misses. Go on away. Mind your own business, whatever it might be."

"Right now, I'm making it my business to find Rochelle Jackson," Steven grumbled. "And, by God, I am determined to find her. And, ma'am, if you're hiding her in either of these cabins, I'll be ready to skin your hide, even if you are a lady!"

"Lawdy be!" Priscilla gasped, taking a wide step backwards. She clasped her hands tightly together before her as Steven pushed his way on into the room to survey its interior.

"I'll report you to the captain of this riverboat, young man," Priscilla said in a rush of words, inching her way toward where Rochelle cowered behind the open door.

"That's fine with me," Steven growled. "He and I are the best of friends. He rode with me during the war. He is the reason I'm traveling on the riverboat. He convinced me it was the best way to forget the last several years of war. The river has a way of calming a person's soul."

He stood tall and threatening over Priscilla. "But right now, I feel anything but calm," he growled, placing his hands on his hips. "After a few inquiries I found out that you are a servant to a red-haired woman. Is that so?"

Rochelle was dying a slow death, again taken by his gentle drawl, still gentle, even though he was angry.

Now realizing how foolish it was to try and delay their finally meeting face to face again, she boldly stepped out from her hiding place and watched him turn to face her, his piercing blue eyes reaching clean into her soul, it seemed.

He surprised her by grabbing her by the wrist to guide her forcibly toward the door. "Steven, what are you doing?" she softly cried.

When he didn't answer, Priscilla came rushing after them. "Let my misses go!" she cried. Her fists began assaulting Steven's arm.

Steven ignored both Priscilla and Rochelle's cries of protests.

"I'll tell the authorities!" Priscilla cried. "I don't care if you *are* best friends with this here captain, there has to be some proper authority on board to take care of scoundrels like you!"

Rochelle felt a desperation rising inside her. She knew what Steven wanted. He wanted private conversation with her and she knew that he had the right to ask this of her after their intimate evening together. She had to convince Priscilla that everything would be all right . . . that Steven was not going to hurt her in any way. But how?

Then she saw Jolene out of the corner of her eye. She turned and faced her as Steven continued to half drag her down the corridor. "Tell your mama, Jolene," she cried. "Tell her everything. She has to know."

"Yas'm," Jolene choked, wringing her hands fitfully.

Rochelle then focused her full attention on her struggles with Steven. "Damn it, Steven," she fussed. "Let me go. This isn't necessary. I will go peacefully."

"Yes, I know," he growled. "Rochelle, I'm not going to give you the chance to get away this time. If I have to tie you to me to be assured that you don't disappear again, I will."

"I can explain, Steven," she said, wincing as he tightened his hold on her wrist.

"I'm sure you can," he snarled. "You've had enough time to come up with an answer."

"But what I have to tell you is true," she said, crying out in fear when he shoved her on into another cabin. Sunlight poured in from an open door which led out onto a private terrace. Clothes were strewn around the room, and his huge bed was in disarray. Her cheeks burned with the thought of being in the same room with him, and so near a bed. If he wished, he could throw her on the bed and take her, and no one would be the wiser. Perhaps that was his plan! He seemed angry enough to have forgotten his gentlemanly ways.

Steven released his hold on her and shut and latched the cabin door, then swung around and looked down at her, his eyes filled with pain. "I've many questions to ask," he said thickly. "The prime one is, who the hell is Anthony Oliver? Why are you in a cabin, a cabin assigned to an Anthony Oliver, when he is not a passenger himself on this boat?"

Rochelle smiled nervously up at him. . . .

Nine

"Who is Anthony Oliver?" Steven persisted, trying to force his eyes from the sight of her, having once thought that he would never see her again. When she appeared on the boat's deck, he thought she had been a figment of his imagination: he hadn't even been able to move, the shock had been so intense.

But after he had regained full composure and had watched her walk away, he had known that she was real, and he had to see her, to ply her with all of his many questions. And he had to see her for even more than that: his nights had been hellish torture without her. He had found in her something that he had never found in any other woman. He had found in her bewitching arms a pleasure so powerful that he had known no other woman would ever fill the void that she had left in his life.

"Anthony?" Rochelle said softly, gliding on away from him, shaken by his intense stare. "How do I tell you, Steven?"

Steven went to her and again grabbed her by a wrist, swinging her around and glowering down at her. "Tell me what?" he growled. "What are you finding so hard to say to me? Why would anything be hard to confess to me? You cared so little for the time we spent together that you even chose to run away from me. Were you afraid of your feelings? Or had you used me for your own selfish purpose?"

Rochelle blanched. She gasped. Her knees became weak and her fingers began to tremble. "That's a terrible thing to say," she said in a rush of words. "I am not guilty of anything as profound as that, Steven . . . truly I am not."

"Then what? Why did you choose me to seduce you? Was it to make it easier for the next man . . . perhaps a man you were planning to marry? Are you already wed? To this man Oliver?"

Rochelle lowered her eyes. The time had come to begin the first steps of her little game. In only a matter of moments, she would know if she had failed . . . or if he would get entangled in her web of deceit. She had waited forever, it seemed, for this moment. She had thought it would happen in Montana, but perhaps now would even be better. At least he wouldn't have to come face-to-face with Anthony for a while. It could spell disaster should Steven confront Anthony in any way, possibly even to fight over her. If he cared even that much for her. . . .

"Anthony Oliver is the man I plan to marry," she blurted out. Her insides were chilled when she saw a mixture of anger and hurt fuse in his eyes. A part of her wanted to inflict pain upon him and another part of her wanted to reach out to touch him, to melt in his embrace.

But all she knew was that she should have only one goal as far as he was concerned. She must remember why she had sought him out in the first place at Colonel Ellsworth's funeral. If she could keep that memory in mind, surely this wouldn't be so hard to carry out to the end. . . .

Steven dropped her wrist as if it were a hot coal. He turned his back to her and walked determinedly across the cabin and out onto his private terrace. Rochelle didn't know what to do next. She had expected for him at least to say something . . . even to shout at her. But not this . . . a silent treatment.

She stood for a moment trying to get the courage to follow him. Running her fingers through her hair, smoothing it back away from her ears, she waited for her heartbeat to slow.

But then finally she felt strong enough to approach him. She would not let it end like this. She hadn't yet been given a chance to fully explain to him. Though it was all going to be half-truths, it had to be said to him, and he had to accept it as truth.

With her head held high, she moved on out onto the terrace and eased quietly next to him at the rail. They were standing almost at water level, close to the paddlewheel. Here and there the sun capped the peaks of the water yellow in the wake of the boat's churning. Everywhere else, the river was a slate gray.

"You didn't let me tell you everything," Rochelle said softly, edging closer to him, smelling the masculine aroma of bay rum and cigars.

"I know," he said huskily. "I wanted to absorb what you did say before hearing any more, Rochelle."

"Anthony Oliver is paying my way to Montana," she continued. "You see, I am what you call a mail-order bride, the same as bought and paid for. Now do you understand why I am in a cabin assigned to Anthony Oliver?"

"I don't think I will ever understand it," he said in a strained voice. "You're so young. Why would you of all people have to be bought and paid for? You could have your pick of men. You know damn well I would've married you."

"No, I didn't know that," she said, again lowering her eyes. "I thought you had seen me as a whore, someone who could not be respected. I let you seduce me so easily, Steven. I even encouraged the seduction; you know that."

"Yes, I know. And I have never been able to understand that," he growled, "as I don't understand why you left that night without even a goodbye."

"I felt guilty for having been so easily bedded," Rochelle said, her green eyes wide and innocent as she looked up at him. She was flooded by desirous feelings for him again and she hated herself for this weakness. Why did he affect her so? Oh, damn it, why him?

His slow grin was absolutely captivating. If he should take her in his arms, there would be no way to say no to anything that he asked of her. There was no denying her feelings when they were with her day and night, troubling not only her waking hours, but also her restless sleep.

Then she realized that he was grinning, not frowning. This had to mean that he accepted her explanations and that his coldness was melting, slowly but surely.

"Rochelle, you know that I did not think ill of you over what we shared that night," he said thickly, taking her hands in his. "I understand needs. Mine were as great as yours." Then his grin faded. "But I will always wonder why you chose me that night."

"Steven, if not you, no one," she murmured. "It was a sudden attraction. I don't know why it was at that moment that I decided to give up my innocence so easily. But why question it? Didn't you ever do anything in life that confused you afterwards?"

Steven remembered the many troubled moments he had had during the war. So often he had acted by instinct alone, mainly as a means of survival. So often he had wished that there had been another way . . . so lives could have been spared.

Yes, he understood how one could wonder. . . .

"All right," he said. "I won't question you further about that. But I have to question this mockery of a marriage that you seem bound to. Surely you aren't serious. You can't marry a man you've never met before."

Rochelle's cheeks flooded with color. She looked away from him, then back up and into his eyes. "I saw no other way," she said softly. "I am alone in the world. I have no living relatives; I had no other choice. It was either marry this man, or live alone and fight off the undesirable men who seemed continually to be at my door."

"God!" Steven gasped. "You poor darling. I never thought that it could be so hard for a woman alone. But of course, you would want to have a man around for protection."

Rochelle smiled smugly to herself, finally seeing that she had gotten her point across, though it was one that was only a lie.

"But Rochelle, now that I've found you, you don't have to marry that other man," Steven said, reaching to frame her face between his hands. "Marry me. Together we'll live on my ranch in Montana. It would be the same as a new beginning for the both of us."

"I can't, Steven," Rochelle murmured. "I made a commitment. I can't back down. Anthony is a warm, sincere man. I must do as promised. Remember . . . he has paid my way to Montana. Even the luxury cabin that I travel in was paid for by him. It would be deceitful of me to accept all of this, then when I arrive in Montana, marry you instead of him."

"Well, we will see about that when we get to Montana," he growled. "And I think it commendable of you to be so honest about this. If I had sent for a woman, I would want her to be as forthright as you."

He drew her into his arms. "But I plan to fight for you once we arrive in Montana," he grumbled. "No matter how long it takes to make this man understand, I will fight for you and win your hand in the end."

Rochelle smiled to herself. Steven was walking straight into her trap. Then her smile faded. Or was it she, walking into his?

But nothing mattered at this moment, for he had drawn her fully against his powerful frame and was setting her aflame with the heat of his lips. As they fully possessed her and his hands held her firmly against him, she felt her body growing feverish and let the euphoria enfold her.

Twining her arms about his neck, she returned his kiss with a passion. When his fingers moved slowly over a breast, caressing it through the thin cotton fabric of her dress, a low moan of desire rose from the depths of her being and she knew that she wanted him . . . fully wanted him. . . .

With more of a purpose than just to kiss her, he drew his lips away from her. His eyes were glazed with desire. He swept her fully up and into his arms and began carrying her back into the privacy of his cabin. Rochelle placed her cheek on his chest, now afraid to look up into his eyes, fearing that he would see just how deep-seated this need for him was. But she could feel the furious pounding of his heart against his chest and understood just how much he desired her. It only seemed right, this desire . . . this passion that they felt for one another. Everything else in life would just have to wait for a while. There were more important needs to be fulfilled in this cabin. . . .

A delicious shiver raced across her flesh as Steven's fingers went to the buttons at the back of her dress and he began to release them, even before he had had her on the bed.

"Steven, I don't know," she said in a whisper, almost swallowed whole by her own nervous heartbeats.

"Rochelle, you do know—what is between us is meant to be," he said hoarsely. "It was meant for us to be together."

He stopped in mid-step and his mouth gaped open. "Lord, Rochelle," he gasped. "I didn't even ask. Where in Montana is this man waiting for you?"

Rochelle smiled at him, hoping that he could not read anything into her smile. Yet when she spoke the name Giltedge, what would his reaction be?

Then her own smile faded. She hadn't even thought to ask him if he was definitely settling in Giltedge! Perhaps they were both in for a rude awakening!

"Giltedge," she blurted.

Steven gaped down at her. "Giltedge?" he mumbled. "Lord, Rochelle, what a coincidence. That's where I'm headed. How can it be?"

"It's a small world, I guess," she shrugged. Then she cuddled against his chest again. "Steven, don't you see how lucky we are? We are going to be neighbors." She only hoped that Anthony's land wasn't too far from Steven's. She had yet to confide in Anthony about her scheme to spoil Montana for Steven. One day she knew she would be forced to, but until then, she would enjoy tormenting Steven in secret.

"You little wench," Steven laughed. "So much about you speaks of mystery. What is it, Rochelle? Why do our lives continually cross? It's as though it was planned."

"It's destiny, Steven." She smiled, "Just destiny. Why not take advantage of it? Surely it was meant to be, or why else would we be on this riverboat at the same time?"

"That's exactly what I mean," he said, carrying her to the bed.

"Why are you on this riverboat?" she mumbled. Then she said, "Oh, yes. You said something about being acquainted with the captain."

"I needed time to put my life together," he said, frowning. "There's so much to forget about these past four years, Rochelle. So much tragedy . . . so much death. On this boat I feel completely at peace with myself."

"Until now? Until with me, I hope," she purred, reaching to unbutton his shirt.

"Until now," he said huskily, easing her down onto the mussed bed. He stretched out beside her, his hands lowering her dress from her shoulders. And when her petticoat was also lowered, his lips went to a nipple and swept down over it.

His tongue flicked, and Rochelle was going wild with pleasure. She placed her hands to his chest and slowly eased her fingers beneath his shirt at his shoulders and lifted it up and away from his muscled torso.

"I've needed you for so long," he whispered, his hands cupping her breasts, his lips now trailing kisses of fire downward, across the flatness of her abdomen. "I didn't think I would ever see you again. Are you truly here with me?"

"Steven," she laughed, "surely you feel the heat rising in my flesh and see the pounding of my pulse in the hollow of my throat. I'm real, every inch of me.

Please love me. I no longer worry about what I may think of myself later. Only now matters. . . ."

She lifted her hips and let him undress her. And when she lay completely nude before his feasting eyes, she felt a sudden shyness, realizing this was only the second time for her to be with a man in such a sensual way. Could it be the same as the first? She would never forget the delicious spinning in her head that coincided with the moment when they both reached the heights of rapture. If he was able to bring her to that joyous pinnacle again, she knew she would never be able to deny him anything—she would forever become a slave to his magic touch.

When he again began worshipping her with his lips, Rochelle felt as though she might explode with the exquisite feelings that he aroused inside her. She reached a hand to his hair and wove her fingers through the golden mass, following his head as it lowered. And when his tongue caressed her most sensitive spot, Rochelle teased and tried to pull away.

Pushing herself up on an elbow, she looked down and questioned him with her eyes as he looked up at her.

"Steven, what you just did," she whispered, her face flushed hot with embarrassment. "Surely that is . . . wrong. . . ."

Steven let his fingers explore where she was denying his lips and watched her eyes take on a drugged glaze. When she stretched back onto the bed, he again tested her by letting his lips now seek out her bud of passion. And this time, when she only stiffened and lay waiting, he lowered his mouth closer and tasted fully of her sweetness.

Rochelle's head began spinning; she could feel a sweet pain where his lips were invading her. His hands stroked her legs and then moved along the sensitive inside of her thighs as his tongue and lips continued to thrill her.

And when she suddenly felt a soft explosion of passion between her thighs, she was surprised and elated at the same time. She looked down at Steven, now seeing him rising away from her, a triumphant glint in his eyes as he began undressing.

Rochelle smiled bashfully up at him, feeling his eyes scorching her wherever they traveled anew. She watched him throw his shirt aside, revealing his broad shoulders and the light feathering of hair which led down beneath the waist of his pants. When he placed his thumbs in place and began inching his pants down over his hips, revealing his readiness to her, she felt her face grow even hotter and she had to turn her head away.

Soon she felt the mattress give beneath his weight as he climbed onto the bed. She trembled with ecstasy as one of his hands began to trail down the gentle curve of her side and then around to cup a breast. She sighed with pleasure, and then her breath caught in her throat when he lifted one of his legs up and over and thrust his manhood against the flesh of her leg.

She could feel the heat of his hardened flesh. And when he moved away from her, and to his knees, to straddle her, she couldn't help but reach out and softly touch its largeness before he placed it inside of her.

She watched his eyes burn brighter with desire as she moved her hand slowly up and down the full length of his manhood. She saw how he strangely tensed when her fingers feathered across the tip of his man's strength.

"Enough," he said huskily. "Rochelle, I can stand no more of this. I must have you. Now. . . ."

A liquid fire scorched her as he thrust into her. He tried to be gentle, knowing that surely it would pain her again, since she had only been taken by a man once in this way. And his suspicions rang true when she let out a soft whimper.

But he kissed this cry away, letting his tongue now slowly enter between her lips to taste of her jasmine sweetness there. Slowly he began moving his body up and down, relishing this feeling of her breasts seeming to rise to meet his chest. His hands became urgent over her body, sending silent messages of love with each touch. And as she arched her hips upward to meet his steady thrusts, he buried his lips along the delicate line of her throat.

Now placing his hands beneath the softness of her shapely buttocks, he anchored her fiercely up against him. He could feel her total surrender in the way in which she was sighing, her eyes closed to the rapture building inside her. Her mouth was soft as she searched his lips out and found them. And when she gave him a torrid kiss, his hands sought her breasts and fully cupped them, feeling a tremor building deeply inside him.

Rochelle welcomed the delicious languor floating inside her head. She welcomed the pleasure spreading throughout her body, a strange sort of warmth, as though she were floating on a river, a part of it even herself.

And then her bodies suddenly rippled against each other and soft moans mingled into ecstasy's pleasure, while together they found the ultimate desire shared between man and woman.

Yet Steven didn't release her. His hands and his lips continued to play with her body, as though it were a fine instrument. He caused Rochelle to writhe, again reaching out for what only he could give her. She let her hands discover every muscle of his body. She smoothed them across his toughened buttocks, and then around to the part of his anatomy which could send her senses spiraling at a mere touch against her flesh.

"I will never get enough of you," she brazenly admitted. "Steven, I don't understand this thing that we've found together at all. It can make me lose sight of all that I've been taught in life."

She knew that it made her lose sight of even more than that. She was so easily guided into lovemaking that she quickly forgot how much she should hate him.

"I shall teach you everything about love, if you will let me," he said thickly, brushing a kiss across one of her taut nipples. "We will be on this river for quite some time, Rochelle. Let's be together. I have to convince you that you don't want to give up your whole future to a stranger. You just can't want to marry that man Anthony."

"Please, let's not talk about that now," Rochelle sighed. "Let's just forget for the moment about everything but us. Please, Steven?"

She curled her fingers through his hair, then coaxed his head down, so she could flick her tongue along the beautiful shape of his lips. And then when he pressed them ardently against hers and gave her a hot, passionate kiss, she melted once more into his body as he lowered himself fully over her.

His mouth was hot and sweet. His fingers bit into her waist as he gripped her and made furious, maddening love to her. Rochelle's passions were cresting, her insides were like lava, splashing and rolling hot, scorching her as never before.

And then, as though a magic wand had been waved